GIVE ME REASON

THE REASON SERIES
BOOK ONE

GIVE ME REASON

THE REASON SERIES
BOOK ONE

ZOEY DERRICK

ISBN: 0615889153
ISBN-13: 978-0615889158

THE REASON SERIES is dedicated to all the woman around the world who are or have been victims of domestic violence.

GIVE ME REASON is dedicated to my AMAZING sidekick Rachel and your support, love and overall begging has kept me going.

PROLOGUE

An angel is he
Alone in this world
With the wealth of three
He'll meet his true love
Answering her song
His wings he will grow
His heart will respond
Him she will follow
His wife she will be
Two joined making three

What had at first appeared to be a faint birthmark slowly morphed into something more. The lines became more defined. Smooth to the touch but appearing shadowed, three-dimensional. And they seemed to flicker, to dance, to be alive.

In the beginning, the lines grew quickly. It took his mother years to realize that they weren't merely random, that they appeared to form a shape or pattern. Of what, it was hard to tell.

Doctors could never explain it because they could never see it; the lines remained a concern with his mother throughout his childhood. Then, when he was eight, the lines stopped changing.

They remained the same until tragedy struck: He'd been helpless to save his family. The changes began anew, with the lines morphing and becoming more pronounced over time. Soon they started sending tingling sensations across his skin. Sensations that were rare and seemingly random.

Until today.

Normally he'd be able to go about his day without too much trouble from the markings on his back. But over the course of today's celebrations — groundbreaking on a new condo project his company has invested in — the pulsing prickles have gone from an irritating nuisance to downright painful. Finding the sensation to be too much to handle around other people, he leaves the cocktail social he's been attending.

When he steps out the front door, he finds his driver.

"G'day, sir. Done so soon?"

"Aye," he says, looking at his driver. Just as the car door opens, the left side of his body hums harder and faster, pulsating, and a strong tugging sensation pulls on his arm. He stops, unsure what to make of it. The tugging has him curious. "I'm going to go for a walk."

"Sir," the driver says and closes the door.

"Stay close, though," he says, and turns to his left.

The moment he takes a step in the direction of the tug, the hum across his back dims slightly. After a couple of pulses and another step, the sensation spreads across his back in a starburst from between his shoulders. Another step and the pulse increases – marginally, but it's stronger still.

Another and another.

With each passing step the sensation gradually increases. After about three blocks it's starting to become painful. He sags under the heavy weight of the pain he is beginning to feel, which forces him to slow down.

Up ahead, the word *diner* is shadowed backwards across the sidewalk. His eyes flicker up to the source of the shadow: light pouring through the windows behind large letters stickered on glass. Normally he wouldn't have even noticed the rundown restaurant, but the hum in his back has turned to pulsing again, as if in excitement or anticipation.

With each step he takes, the pulse radiates across his entire body, the sensations across his back pushing him forward.

He glances up the sidewalk, and there's a flash of bright white followed by ghosted stars. Rubbing at his eyes, he sputters, "What the hell?" He opens his eyes again, looks from side to side to check that his vision has returned to normal. His gaze lands upon what he'd subconsciously seen the first time.

Bright white light surrounding a red-haired, blue-eyed angel. Gorgeous.

The pulsing turns to a pleasurable buzzing sensation as the young lass walks toward the diner and goes inside. Her shoulders are slumped protectively around her body. He cocks his head, puzzled.

Suddenly his mind fills with a quick series of images — blurred and unrecognizable, but he has a sense of what he needs to do now, though it's not clear to him what's driving the need.

He takes a step and the hum ceases. Feeling the need to test his invisible guide, he takes a step backward. It roars across his skin in response. He turns around, takes a step away from the diner, and there's a stab of pain between his shoulder blades so sharp it causes his knees to buckle.

Quickly, he turns and heads back toward the diner. The sensation levels out to a pleasurable buzzing as he closes in on the restaurant.

He can see *her* through the window. She's heading toward a door in back, bright blue and white light engulfing her form. It's beautiful. And so is she.

ONE

The chilly October air has me huddled inside my hoodie. My feet are swollen and sore, and I'm flat-out exhausted, but I slowly stagger into the diner that I started working at about a month ago.

Waitressing at Garrison's Diner is far from my ideal job, but what can I say? It's a job, and the tips are...well, they're tips. I've managed to survive. For now. It's Tuesday, usually a day off for me, but Nyssa, one of the other girls who works here, needed the evening off, so I stepped up to take her shift. Right now, every little bit helps.

"Hi, Viv," Laura calls from behind the counter as the bell on the front door announces my entrance.

"Hi, Laura," I say back, fake enthusiasm in my voice.

"How are you doing today?"

"Fine, I think." She gives me a quizzical look. The same look she gives me every time I give her that answer. I just nod slightly at her.

Laura is in her mid-fifties and has been working in this diner for at least the last thirty years. Her hair is nearly all gray, and the wrinkles in the corners of her eyes only appear when she smiles, which makes me think her smiles are genuine. She is very warm and motherly. Maybe this is why I find her so hard to handle some days.

I head toward the back to stow my bag, shed my hoodie and change into my stark white tennis shoes: a uniform requirement to go with your typical diner garb of a pink and white smock that flatters no figure.

I slide my hoodie off — not that the sweatshirt does much against the chilly Minneapolis rain — and notice the small bump rising from between my hips. I shiver. I've lost so much weight since the trip to the hospital two months ago that everything seems bigger and more pronounced on my body. My knees seem huge compared to the rest of my leg. My collarbones, shoulders and ribs are eerily prominent.

Looking back down at the bump, I realize that my boss, crabby old Bartie, is going to have a field day when he figures this out. He's quick to think about the impact his staff may have on him and his precious diner. Thank goodness it's covered by my apron. For now.

I take a seat on the bench in front of the four lockers in the employee area and sigh. "How did we get here?" I say to no one. I can't believe that it's been two months since that asshole put me in the hospital. With each passing day going a little more quickly than the last, I'm finally beginning to feel more like myself, but the overly friendly, bubbly personality that I used to have after I got away from my mom is still lost inside.

But I don't want to dwell on it anymore; I know I'll just end up in a crying heap on the floor. I take a deep breath and stand. Tying my apron around my waist, I stuff my hoodie and bag into the locker and head back out to the dining room, grabbing my timecard along the way and punching into the ancient time clock. It's four in the afternoon. I can already tell it's going to be a long night.

When I step back out into the diner, I'm greeted by the classic fifties diner décor in black, white, chrome and red.

It no doubt looked great at one time, I suppose. Red faux leather booth benches, white tables with chrome trim that now sport a weathered, well-used look. On top of every table, jukeboxes and bottles of ketchup and mustard sit alongside sugar packets and napkins in old-school metal holders. The black and white checkers on the floor continue up the side of the counter that separates the dining room from the kitchen. The countertop itself is white with cherry red trim.

"Viv, there's a gentleman in the corner that just came in. Would you mind?" Laura says as soon as I clear the swinging door. I'm pretty sure Laura makes a point of giving me as many tables as she can because she knows I need the money. It's either that or laziness. Either way works fine for me; I'll take what I can get.

"Sure." I reach for a menu and head over toward the far side of the diner.

As I approach table twelve, I realize that its sole occupant is wearing a rather expensive-looking suit and tie. Having come from trailer parks in the middle of Podunk Nowhere, Everywhere, my idea of an expensive suit is something you'd find at JCPenney. But this...this looks to be more than that.

"Good afternoon," I say, my southern accent echoing through the diner. You usually can't hear the accent, but it seems to come out when I'm trying to be friendly. I set the menu down in front of him.

"Thank you." His voice is deep, raspy. A bit of an accent rolling off his tongue. He grabs the menu and opens it. I cringe internally when I notice something stuck to the front cover. Ugh, that's so disgusting.

I shake off my mortification at the dirty menu and tell him, "Today's special is roasted turkey, mashed 'tatoes, gravy, with a side of veg'table medley."

I see him shake his head. "Would you eat that?" His question throws me off guard and I scowl at him. Right now I'm so hungry I'd eat a cow. Raw.

"Of course," I say softly. He is quick to catch the reverence in my voice about the mention of food. His head snaps up, hard, and he looks straight at me. His eyes are a deep blue-green. Ocean-like. Piercing straight into me. His gaze has me feeling like all my secrets are pouring from my body. It's unnerving and I try to tear my eyes away, but it's like he's got me under a spell. After a few heartbeats he releases me from his stare.

"So the special is not your favorite thing on the menu. What would you eat?" he asks, his voice rasping again. I still can't place the accent, but it's definitely not American. Irish maybe.

"The barbecue bacon burger is really good. With fries." I lean in a little and whisper slightly, so I'm not overheard by Radar-Ears Laura. "Avoid the slaw," I advise him. Having lived in Georgia a good portion of my life, I can say with authority that this slop Bartie calls coleslaw is a travesty. He nods in response and I find it hard to pull away. His scent has registered on me and I'm immediately drawn to him even more. It's warm, clean. He smells of leather and a delicious cologne. Committing the scent to memory, I back away. "You want a few minutes?" I ask.

"No," he says, sharply, and with a strong sense of authority. "I'll have the barbecue bacon burger, no slaw." I smile. "Fries, a Coke, and a side of mayonnaise."

I write down his order, though I don't need to. It's committed to memory, but my ass-hat of a boss has this thing about proof. He seems to think everyone is stealing from him. "Anything else?"

"No." That authority is back in his voice. It's strange: His tone isn't threatening or demanding, it just projects a sense of confidence and maybe even a little cockiness. Nonetheless, something tells me that this man knows what he wants and is not to be messed with.

"Okay, darlin', I'll be back with your Coke," I say and turn toward the counter. As I walk back, I can feel his piercing eyes on me. I'm tempted to turn around just to show him I'm not one to be intimidated by a stare-down, but I don't give him the satisfaction. Besides, he might get the wrong impression and think I'm flirting with him. Friendly maybe, but nothing more than that; I'm in no position to be flirting with someone intentionally.

"You were over there a long time," Laura says to me as I reach for a glass.

"He was having a hard time deciding what he wanted to eat," I say back, trying really hard to not be rude.

"Oh reeeaaallyyy..." she says, dragging out the last word.

I look up at her, shocked by her reaction. "What?" I say.

"You mean to tell me you weren't checking him out while you were over there?" I just shake my head and go back to filling the glass with ice and Coke. "Well he was sure checking you out."

"What's your point, Laura?" I say, and she glares at my tone.

"My point, Vivienne, is that he was checking you out and you flat-out ignored him. He's gorgeous. What is your problem?"

My eyes prickle with tears. My problem is that I'm broken and damaged and I don't need some deranged man to lust after right now. "I have a lot on my mind," I say out loud. Laura is insanely nice and sweet and — lest we forget — motherly. She doesn't need to know all the gory details.

"You always have a lot on your mind. You're twenty-two years old, what more can be on your mind than going out with friends and having a good time?"

Oh, if you only knew. "You know that's not who I am," I say as I turn back toward Mr. Suit. I look up in his direction. He most certainly is watching me, his eyes a bright light in his otherwise dark features.

I finally take a moment to really look at him. He looks to be not much older than me, actually. Maybe twenty-five or twenty-six? His hair is black, slicked back except for a stray strand falling into his eyes. His jaw is hard and sharp, leading into a very strong, square chin. His lips are a soft pink, full, and he has deep-set, bright blue eyes. There's an intensity to his gaze that has me so transfixed I nearly trip over my own feet as I make my way back to his table.

Damn it, Vivienne, get your head out of your ass, I scold myself as I approach his table. Tripping over my own feet and spilling Coke all down this guy's front is just the kind of thing that would get me fired, and I can't afford to lose this job.

"Can I get you anything else right now?"

"No, I'm good, thanks," he says, his eyes still boring into me with that intense stare.

Luckily for me we get busy, and aside from bringing him his food and his check I manage to pretty much ignore him for the rest of his meal. Which is why it surprises me when I go to clear the table and find a thirty percent tip.

TWO

No sooner do I set foot in the diner the next day for another shift than Mr. Suit from the night before shows up again. Our food is not that good. I can't imagine what on earth is bringing him back here again.

Laura takes to seating him, and I, of course, get left with the table. Tonight he asks me how I am, and we converse a little bit. Nothing too exciting. He orders the same thing as last night, and again I don't get to spend much time with him because we get busy.

He pays his tab, gives me another thirty percent tip and leaves.

Finally Thursday rolls around and I'm beyond exhausted. I've worked every day since Sunday. But I do what I need to in order to survive. I make squat for an hourly wage, and I lose a lot of money when it comes to tips paid with credit or debit cards because they're taxed through my meager paycheck. But luckily most of our customers pay cash, and I usually manage to walk out with about fifty dollars a week.

I find myself slightly disappointed when I'm in the diner for more than an hour and Mr. Suit from the last two nights hasn't shown up yet. Then I beat myself up for actually hoping he would come by again.

I head off to the back to grab some more silverware for the wrapping Laura and I are working on, and when I come back, I nearly drop the tub all over the floor.

Sitting at table twelve is none other than Mr. Suit himself. Looking as dashing as ever tonight in another suit and tie. If this man can afford to dress like that, why on earth does he eat here?

I look to Laura, who nods encouragingly, and I head on over to the table. Ironically enough, he has the same menu from the other night, the one I'd forgotten to clean. Obviously no one else has cleaned it, either.

"Hi there. How are you tonight?"

"Great, thanks. I'll have the same - if you remember." He smiles.

"Barbecue bacon burger, fries and a Coke?"

He smiles again. "You got it."

"I'll be right back."

After what seems like an eternity, I finally make it back to his table. The dirty menu is staring me in the face once again. "Here you go," I say, setting down his glass and pulling a straw from my apron. I reach for the menu, determined to go and clean it off. I realize as I reach out that my hand is shaking. This fact does not go unnoticed by Mr. Suit. He tries to reach for my hand. I pull it back quickly, clutching the menu.

"Do I make you nervous?" he asks in his usual stern voice. I shake my head. "You're shaking like a leaf." I look quickly at his face. His jaw is set into a hard line, his lips pursed. "When was the last time you ate anything?"

"This morning," I say quickly. It's true: I ate a hot dog for breakfast this morning. Cold, straight from the refrigerator.

"You should eat something," he says, attempting to soften his tone.

"Thank you, sir." I watch his nostrils flare. "However, I assure you, I'm fine."

"It's not you I'm worried about," he says, staring coldly at me.

"Excuse me?" There's no way. How could he possibly know?

"Forget it. I shouldn't have intruded."

I try to gather my thoughts. "Can I get you anything else?"

"Yes," he says. His eyes rake up and down my body from head to toe. Rest assured, he's not seeing anything worth looking at twice. I wait patiently for him to go on, but nothing comes.

"What would that be?"

"A duplicate of what I just ordered. For yourself."

I shake my head. "It's not allowed."

"And you need to eat," he all but growls at me.

"I appreciate your concern, but I can*not* afford to lose my job. So, thank you for your offer, however, I respectfully decline. Now if there is nothing else I can get *you*," I say, adding emphasis, "I will be back in just a few minutes with your food."

I turn quickly before he can trap me again with his stare. The look on his face is hard, unyielding. Something tells me that he's going to find a way for me to lose this argument.

When I return to the counter, Laura starts in with the Spanish Inquisition about my conversation with Mr. Suit.

"He saw my hand shake when I picked up his menu. Then tried to order a burger for me to eat."

"When was the last time you ate?" she asks.

"Jeez, stop. This morning, alright?"

"No, Viv, it's not alright. You need to eat, you're nothing but skin and bones."

I roll my eyes at her and turn to grab the washrag so that I can clean this stupid menu. "One meal won't solve that problem," I mutter bitterly.

"So let him buy you a meal," she says. I shake my head stubbornly. "I won't tell Bart."

"No, Laura. You know damn well he will find out, and when he does he will think I conned a nice customer into buying me food. It's not worth losing my job over."

"You say that as though your life means nothing," she says dryly.

I shrug. Lately I'm not sure how much I care about myself or my life.

"Damn it, Vivienne, what the heck is wrong with you?"

I just shake my head. "Stop. Please, Laura. I get it. I'll try and eat."

She just shakes her head and goes about her business. Antonio hits the bell on the pass-through, telling me that Mr. Suit's food is ready. I go grab a tray, wipe it off with the rag and put the plates on it, hoping and praying I don't get caught in his stare, trip and fall on my face and make an ass of myself on the way back to his table.

I make my way there, feeling a little more confident because I haven't actually looked at him. I quickly place his burger and fries on the table, followed by the bowl of mayonnaise. "Anything else?" I ask, not looking at him.

"Will you join me?"

"I..." I shake my head. "I can't."

Suddenly I feel a hand at my back, causing me to jump slightly, and Laura comes into my peripheral vision. "Is everything alright?" she says quietly and quickly.

"I asked her to join me," Mr. Suit says to Laura. Fantastic.

"Oh, what a fabulous idea. Vivienne, why don't you take a break," she says, more as an order than as a request.

"I just started. I don't–"

She cuts me off. "You're fine. Have a seat. No one else in here anyway," she says and walks away.

I look toward the man in the booth. He has a smirk of satisfaction on his face. "Now you have no excuse. Take a seat."

I huff loudly. I want to protest and throw a fit, but I have to admit, I'm curious. And, I realize with a sigh, I really am hungry. I concede to his demand and slide in across from him. As soon as I sit down, he pushes his food in my direction. I push it back and shake my head.

He pushes it at me again. I look at Laura, who nods and mouths, "Go ahead."

"What about you?" I say quietly.

"What about me?" he retorts.

"This is your food," I say. I'm trying to be tough, but the food in front of me smells so good. My mouth begins to water and I swallow back the saliva.

"I've eaten since this morning, for one. And for two, I think your co-worker over there has already placed an order for me." He nods at me. "So, now you have no excuses. Eat." His tone is gentle, but it still feels like an order.

With the smell of food in my nostrils, I'm too hungry to argue anymore. I reach for the ketchup, squirt it all over the fries and dive in.

THREE

Somewhere around the last of my French fries, Laura shows up with another plate for Mr. Suit, whose name I have yet to learn. She nods with approval at the fact that only half of the burger is left. "Do you want anything else?" she says.

I roll my eyes.

He scowls.

I shake my head.

"Water. And two more Cokes," he says as he hands his now-empty glass to Laura.

"I'll be right back." And she's off toward the counter.

I stare at the last half of my burger and debate whether or not to finish it, but then my stomach rumbles and I pick it up. Just as I lean in to take a bite, I see him staring at me again. "What?" I say around my burger, and he smirks at me.

"I'm not sure I've ever seen anyone eat with such purpose before. Like you're eating your last meal. Why don't you eat?"

Really? Bottom line, I can barely afford the hot dogs I do have. But there's no way I'm going to tell him that. "I'm just not hungry."

"That, Vivienne, is bullshit," he says with such an edge to his voice and such a straight face that I nearly drop my burger.

"What the hell do you care?" I snap. "I'm a waitress in some random diner, and you feel sorry for me, so you buy me a meal." Roughly setting the burger back on the plate, I slide to the end of the booth and stand up. "Don't worry about my food, I'll find a way to pay for it," I say and attempt to storm off, but suddenly the room is spinning. I feel my body start to sway, and the floor rises fast. I close my eyes — bracing for impact — and black out.

"We need to call an ambulance," I hear a male voice say. A voice that seems familiar, but...

"She'll put up a huge fight." That voice I know. It's Laura.

I feel arms tighten around me. "Vivienne." A hand strokes along my arm. "Vivienne." It's the male, Mr. Suit. My eyes flutter. "Vivienne, are you alright?"

I nod, I think. Or at least I intend to, but I can't quite tell if I have actually moved. "Ye—yes," I croak.

"Thank God," he groans, and my eyes open. Our gazes meet. His expression is soft, concerned. His eyes are warm, liquid. I feel his hand slide along my arm again. The sensation sends shivers across my skin and I squirm.

"Wh—" I breathe. "What happened?"

"You tried to storm off in a big bad huff, and I caught you on your way down." He's smiling at me. "Not my usual effect on women." I try to smile but instead I end up rolling my eyes. He laughs. "Yeah, you'll be alright."

I squirm, attempting to get up. He helps me sit upright, and Laura is quick to hand me a Coke. "You need the sugar," she says as she puts the straw to my mouth.

"I got it," Mr. Suit says as he takes it from Laura.

Laura smiles at me, then stands and heads back toward the counter.

I take another sip and I feel myself slowly coming back to normal. "Thank you."

His hand moves toward my face. I flinch and his expression changes, becomes instantly harder and more concerned. I shake my head and tuck the strand of loose hair behind my ear. I look up at him again. His eyes are warming, concern still etched in his features, and I shake my head again. "Sorry," I say.

He cocks his head to the side. "For?"

"Passing out. Flinching." *Existing,* I add in my head. His hand slowly strokes my arm. His touch is warm, soft. A tender gesture. Tears prick my eyes again. I turn my head away from him, instead looking down at the floor.

"What's your name?" I ask.

"Mikah."

"Well, Mikah, thank you for the meal. I truly appreciate it." I move to stand up. The flood of embarrassment I feel right now is overwhelming, and I just want to get away from him as quickly and gracefully as I can manage.

"Let me help you." He stands up quickly and then bends back down to help me come slowly to my feet. Once I'm upright, he steadies me so that I don't fall over again.

"I'm fine. Really." I still can't meet his gaze. "I'm going to go clean up. Why don't you sit back down and eat your burger." I start to walk away, gingerly, making sure that my head is not going to start spinning again. I catch a glimpse at the clock as I pass through the swinging door. Seven-thirty. Jeez, tonight is going fast. How long was I passed out?

Heading into the bathroom, I take care of business, then take a look in the mirror. "Jesus." I look like hell. There are deep hollows around my eyes, my cheekbones are way more pronounced and my cheeks look bruised. My bright red curly hair is pulled back into a tight bun, except for the strand Mikah was trying to move when I flinched. God, I can't believe I thought he was going to hit me.

Damn it, Riley really did a number on me. I hadn't realized that his actions would have such long-term effects. I've managed to stay away from him — from men in general — since he put me in the hospital, and I haven't really had to face any of it.

Riley was good at nothing except using me as a punching bag. A habit that nearly killed me two months ago. After Riley put me in the hospital, a social worker got involved and set me up with a place to live and a job. Which is how I ended up working here at the diner.

Pulling myself back together, I straighten my uniform, wash my hands and run cool water over my face before heading back out through the swinging door and into the dining room. My eyes scan the room. With the exception of Laura behind the counter, it's empty. I feel hope rush out of me as I realize that Mikah is no longer in the diner. Turning to Laura, I ask her, "Did he leave?" I can hear the disappointment in my voice and hope Laura doesn't catch it.

She just nods, so I grab the tub and head toward the table to clear off our plates. His is untouched; he never ate his food. Come to think of it, I never gave him his bill. Damn it all to hell, how am I going to pay for all of this? Irritation courses through me, and I turn back to Laura. "You let him leave without his bill?"

She shrugs. "He said he left the money on the table. I figured he would leave enough to cover it. Lord knows he can afford it." She goes back to wiping down the counter.

I turn back to the table. Man, he really didn't touch his food at all. I place the back of my fingers on top of the fries. They're ice cold. Jeez, how long was I out? I start gathering up the dishes and putting them in the tub. When I go to grab the plate I'd been eating off of, I see that something is sticking out from under it. I go to place the plate in the tub and nearly drop it.

FOUR

Sitting under the plate is a hundred dollar bill with a business card paperclipped to it. But when I pick it up, I realize there's more here than a hundred dollar bill. I pull the paperclip off to find four additional bills folded together — five hundred dollars in all — and a piece of paper. I slide into the booth, my hand covering my mouth and tears streaming down my face.

I suppose I should feel joy or relief about being given this much money, but all I can feel is indignation at the fact that he feels I'm some charity case. I unfold the small piece of paper that was tucked in with the bills. It's a note.

Vivienne,

I'm sure you're angry at this money, but please, don't be. Consider it a tip for a job well done and please, call me. I've attached my card.

-Mikah

I look at his business card. Its elegant silver lettering practically jumps off of the sleek black card.

Mikah Blake – CEO, MSB Enterprises

There is a phone number — maybe an office number — a website, an address downtown and an email address. I flip the card over. On the back, in the same handwriting as the note, are two phone numbers. A cell phone? Home phone?

I shrug and wipe the dampness from my cheeks. I'm not going to call him. I'm going to pay for the meal, take twenty percent for tip and find a way to give him back the rest. Despite the fact that this is enough to cover all of my rent this month, I cannot and will not accept a four hundred and seventy dollar tip from a man that sees fit to feed and take care of me.

The rest of the night passes by slowly, which is normal for a Thursday. We close at midnight and are out the door by five after because we spent the last hour of the shift cleaning everything up. I head out the front door with Laura, and she locks up.

"See you tomorrow," Laura says as I head toward the bus stop at the corner. "You want a ride?" Laura's typical nightly question.

"No, I got it. Thanks," I say and keep walking. It's early enough I can still catch the twelve ten west toward my apartment.

As I wait for the bus, my eyes droop, exhaustion registering. Luckily I only have to wait a few minutes. Al, the driver, opens the door and I climb up.

"Good evening, Ms. Vivienne."

"Hi, Al," I say sleepily as I put my money in the machine.

"How was business?"

I shrug. "Slow, as usual." I turn toward the back of the bus and let out a sigh of relief. It's empty. "Seems pretty slow for you, too, tonight."

"It sure is."

I grab a seat right behind him. Al is getting on in years, but he obviously loves his job. I asked him once why he drives the late night routes, and he said it was so he could see me. But I think it has more to do with protecting us girls that ride at this time of the night. Usually there are several of us on the bus: some traveling home from work, others looking for their next fix. Going anywhere at this hour can be scary. Fortunately for me, my bus stop is just around the corner from my shitty studio apartment in South Minneapolis.

I fight to keep my eyelids open as the bus rumbles along. Almost home. Almost to my mattress.

"Vivienne, honey, you're home," I hear Al say, and my eyes fly open.

"Thanks, Al." I gather up my things and step off the bus.

"Have a good night, Vivienne."

"You too, Al," I say as he closes the door. I watch as he pulls away, and I quickly make my way around the corner without drawing attention to myself. The street is dirty and it smells like trash and rotting food. Graffiti covers the walls around me.

I see my shadow lengthen as a car comes up from behind me, and I pick up the pace a little. Cars on the street this time of night, in this neighborhood, usually mean someone is up to no good. The car passes me as I reach my door. I glance up and see that it is a sleek black Mercedes. I scowl at it. What's a fancy car like that doing in this neighborhood? I push past the blue door and into the entryway and unlock the inner door.

The hallways are an uneven brownish yellow, almost like they're stained with nicotine. Judging from the smell, that's probably exactly what it is. The garbage that lines the baseboards of the entrance and the stairs is disgusting, but tonight I don't have the energy to care.

I shuffle up the stairs to the third floor. When I reach my door, I unlock the two deadbolts, turn the handle and slip into my apartment. I shut the door with my butt and lean back against it.

There is always a sigh of relief when I get home, knowing that I made it safely yet again. I've been harassed more than a few times on the streets and the bus, even in the less than twenty-five feet between the bus stop and the door.

I lock the two deadbolts and the knob and slide the chain. To be honest the door is so flimsy that someone could easily just kick it in, but the locks help me feel a little bit better.

My apartment is one room, a closet, and a bathroom. The kitchen consists of a small oven with a two-burner cook top, a half-size refrigerator, a small counter and sink. A few cupboards lie as empty and as useless as the fridge.

I head to the sink, grab a glass and fill it with water. I swallow it down quickly and refill it. As I drink half of the new glass, I unbutton my uniform with my other hand. When I reach the apron I put the glass down.

My hands slip into the apron pockets, and I feel the wad of cash from Mikah. My heart sinks. I can't keep this. It's not mine, and I'm nobody's responsibility. I walk the two steps over to my bed and fish around for my notebook between the mattress and the pallets that raise my bed off of the floor. I tear a blank piece of paper from the notebook and throw the money, the paper, and a pen from my apron onto the counter.

Then I take off my apron, smock and shoes. Looking down at my semi-naked form, I can see that small bump rising between my hips. It looks bigger tonight, no doubt because I've actually eaten a meal. Trying hard not to dwell on my swelling abdomen and the reasons for my current state of affairs, I shed my bra and panties and stumble into the bathroom. When I release the bun atop my head, the thick, curly red waves fall down my back and tickle my hips.

I turn the water on to the hottest setting possible, hoping like hell that there is some hot water left in the tanks downstairs. After a couple of minutes the water is lukewarm at best. I climb in, praying that it lasts for at least a few minutes before turning ice cold.

It doesn't. I don't waste time and I'm in and out quickly. Shivering, I towel off, turn up the heat a bit and grab my cotton pajama bottoms and a t-shirt full of tiny holes. I pull on the clothes and wrap my hair in the towel. A few more minutes of chattering teeth before I hear the heater kick on. At least that works in this damn place.

I need to write Mr. Blake a note, but it can wait until morning. The shower and shivering have drained me, and I can't stay awake any longer. I don't have to be to work until four tomorrow, so I'll have plenty of time to write the note before heading out.

I climb into bed and shiver again as the cool sheets touch my skin. Pulling the blankets up to my chin, I try and settle into the lumpy, uneven mattress as best I can.

As I close my eyes, the last image my brain conjures up is an image of Mikah bent over me as I woke up from my fainting incident.

FIVE

"No! Stop!"

"I could kill you, bitch! What the fuck? You're such a whore." Smack across the face. He grabs my arms and shakes me. "You little fucking whore. I knew you would do this. I knew you were a no-good bitch." He pushes me away, hard, and I slam into the wall. As I fall to the floor all I can feel is the crack against my skull and...

My eyes fly open. I'm covered in sweat and the blankets are all twisted around my legs. I stare up at the dingy ceiling. Light streams in through the small window by the kitchen. Blinking back tears, I attempt to calm myself down by rubbing absently at my tummy with one hand.

"You asshole," I mutter.

I spent three days in the hospital after that night with a skull fracture, a concussion, severely bruised ribs and a sprained wrist. I was purple and black from head to toe. On the second day I found out that Riley had been arrested and charged with domestic abuse. He was later charged with endangerment when the hospital revealed to the police that I was pregnant. They had said there was a chance that I could lose the baby, but they took good care of me.

Yolanda, a state social worker, asked me if I had anywhere to go. I told her no, and she did what she could to give me a safe place for me to recover after leaving the hospital. Once I was in Amber's Place, Yolanda helped me find this apartment and set me up to meet grouchy Bartie at the diner. Given that I had no experience, he was reluctant to give me a job as a waitress, but he said I had a great smile and gave me a chance, and it all worked out okay in the end. I suppose Laura had something to do with it; she took to me quickly and was very attentive when it came to training me.

My stomach starts doing flips. I pull myself free of the blankets and stumble into the bathroom. At least I make it to the toilet this time.

After I'm done retching, I brush my teeth and run my fingers through my hair. As curly as ever. Looking myself over in the mirror, I notice that a little color has returned to my cheeks and my eyes don't seem as hollow. It must be the burger I ate yesterday, but it'll only last for a day or two and I'll go right back to the way I was.

I head into the kitchen but stop before I get to the fridge, shaking my head. I'm choosing to skip the morning hot dog. Despite having just emptied my stomach, I don't feel hungry. I settle for a glass of water.

I grab the pen and paper and sit on my bed. Pulling the journal out to use as a hard surface on which to write, I start composing my note to Mr. Suit.

Mikah,

Or should I call you Mr. Blake?

While I truly appreciate your gesture yesterday, I cannot accept your outrageous tip. Please accept your change from your meal at the diner last night — you know, the one you didn't eat, and the one you forced on me.

I've always found ways to survive just the way that I am. I don't need your money to make it through.

Thank you,

Vivienne

A little while later, I leave my apartment. I'm dressed as nicely as I can manage in the skirt and blouse I wore to my interview with Bartie and the Mary Jane shoes that were given to me during my stay in the shelter. The outfit is hidden beneath my worn, oversized hoodie. It's colder today than it has been.

My hair is down. I'm hoping that it will make me harder to recognize when I arrive at Mr. Suit's office. I really have no desire to see him again.

But before I can go there, I need to make a stop along the way. I cross the street to wait at the eastbound bus stop. It's still early – about seven thirty – and the street is mostly quiet. The daily commuters are mostly already at work, and the neighborhood crowd hasn't emerged from their houses. There are a few passing cars, but the neighborhood just looks rundown and abandoned compared to other parts of the city.

I'm used to living like this, though. It's the kind of life I've always known. I grew up the only child of a single mom who worked three and four jobs. But she did it more to support her drug habits than to support me. It's amazing that I managed to stay away from drugs.

The bus arrives and I climb up, put my money in the machine and grab a seat about halfway back. First stop, the diner. It's Friday — payday. Then I can run across the street to cash my meager check and head off to my next destination.

After cashing my check, I get back on the bus and head further east to my next destination: Moore's Family Home. I don't usually go to see my mother on Fridays, but I figure that since I'm running downtown today it makes sense to go, and I can just stay in my neighborhood tomorrow.

When I walk in, the lady at the counter greets me by name. Then she tells me, "She's in the game room."

"How is she today?" I ask.

"She seems to be having a good day today. Enjoy your time." This is the typical response when I ask about my mother. I nod, and the buzzer sounds.

I walk quickly through the drab, white-on-white, hospital-style hallway until I reach the game room. When I turn the corner, I see her sitting in a wheelchair facing the window. Her nightgown is light blue, very old and thin at the shoulders. Her gray hair is about shoulder length. She looks years older than the forty-eight that she is. Years of drugs and alcohol have completely destroyed her body. And her mind. Until she moved in here about five years ago, she had never sobered up. Now they have her on all manner of medication for paranoia, bipolar disorder and schizophrenia. Most of the time she's pretty out of it.

"Hi, Momma," I say as I sit in the chair next to her.

She doesn't respond, just keeps staring out the window. This is typically how our visits go. It's better than a bad day; it's not pretty when she's jumpy or freaking out. She can get very violent.

Knowing that I'm taking the money back to Mikah today has me on edge. To top it off, a lot of things from my past that I've worked very hard at suppressing keep floating through my brain. Like the way we moved around from city to city, state to state.

It seemed like every time my mother got a wild hair up her ass we were off. Sometimes in the middle of the night.

Which of course was never a problem: She never let me keep toys, and I only had enough clothes to fill up half of a garbage bag. A few pairs of pants, a couple of t-shirts and a pair of sneakers were usually about it. Even to this day my list of material possessions is so small that I can probably pack everything inside of one box and a trash bag.

Hell, I moved into my apartment with about three days' worth of clothes, two pairs of shoes, my journal — compliments of the psychotherapist at Amber's Place — and my bag. Or purse. Or whatever you want to call it. Since then I've also acquired a small pitcher and a cooking pot. Not that they get much use; I've got nothing to cook.

My tummy rumbles. Maybe I should have had that hot dog before I left.

Momma still isn't saying anything, just staring out the window. Lord knows what she's looking at. Or if she's even looking at anything. Sometimes I think she's just lost inside of her own mind, trying in vain to pull herself out. But then again, that's probably just me hoping. Hoping she will come around. It's wishful thinking, I know, but it is one of the few things that keeps me coming back here time after time.

It's been about five years now that she had her stroke. We had just gotten into Minneapolis from somewhere in Chicago. We didn't stay there long, so I don't remember too much about it. Before Chicago we had been in Ohio, Michigan, New York, Maryland, Georgia - which is where we spent the majority of my younger years – Florida, Alabama and Texas. She told me that we had been in Arizona, California and Nevada when I was really young, but I don't remember it. I don't remember everything about Georgia either, but that is where some of the few brighter highlights of my life happened.

I never went to the same school for a whole year, but I was always enrolled. She found me easier to deal with when I was gone in school for eight hours a day. It meant she was free to do whatever she wanted without me around to bother her.

I was able to graduate from a vocational school shortly after coming to Minneapolis. I managed to test out of all the required classes and then some. I actually scored a seventeen hundred on my SATs — which I was told was beyond awesome — and that I could pretty much attend any school I wanted to. I even had a couple of colleges come after me, but the catch was, I was broke and couldn't afford their tuition. Besides, school wasn't anywhere I needed to be.

It wasn't long after that SAT test that my mom suffered a severe stroke that left the right side of her body useless and put her in the mental state that she is in right now. The stroke was a blessing in disguise. It forced her to detox and sober up, but the flip side is that she can't do much on her own and she's forced to live in this home. But when you break it down, it's better this way.

Better for me, or better for her? That is the question I always find myself trying to answer. The selfish side of me wants to say it's better for me that she's here. Hell, even the non-selfish side of me says it is better for me. Having her here means she's sober and not on the streets. Despite all the times I've been asked why I don't just walk away, I still come here, thinking that maybe my presence brings her some sense of joy. Maybe one day I will find the strength to move on. But today is not that day.

I say my goodbyes, kiss her on the cheek and leave the facility. I need to get downtown and then be back at the diner by four.

The bus drops me off right across the street from Capella Tower. It's a beautiful building, sleek and modern with glass walls and a rounded rooftop. I cross at the crosswalk and head into the building. The entrance is huge, with stone floors and glass-domed ceiling. There is a large directory toward the back, and I head over to it.

I've seen this building a hundred thousand times in the Minneapolis skyline, but this is the first time I've been inside. The elaborate decor makes me feel even poorer than usual, even more out of place.

I finally find MSB Enterprises. It's on floors forty-two through fifty-two. There's an asterisk next to level fifty and a note: *All Visitors Please Report To Level 50.* Well, level fifty it is.

When I get to the bank of elevators, I see signs over several of them indicating which floors they go to. I push the up arrow next to the elevator labeled *42-52.*

Jeez, they even have their own elevator?

I shift nervously from foot to foot while I wait for the elevator to arrive, again conscious of being completely out of my element. When it comes, I can hear voices — male voices — on the inside.

"Oh, no," I breathe, and I slink away toward the back of the hallway, hoping the men will just exit and turn toward the entrance, away from me.

The doors open and six men file out. Five of them head toward the entryway. The sixth gentleman quickly slides past me toward the door at the end of the hallway. Thankfully, I don't recognize any of them as Mr. Suit.

I duck into the elevator and look at the control panel. Above the buttons there's a little sign that reads, *Entry to floors 42-49 prohibited without a key card. Floors 51-52 only accessible from floor 50.* Well, I guess I have no choice but to go to the fiftieth floor. I push the button and lean into the wall, wrapping my arms around my ribcage. After a few moments the elevator starts to chime as we pass every third floor past the twentieth. I watch the numbers rise by threes, wrapping my arms tighter around my chest, nerves taking over.

I regret coming here. I hadn't thought this far ahead, and I don't have a clue how to go about leaving this for him. Maybe there will be a receptionist I can leave the note with.

I suddenly have the urge to see him again, something I hadn't expected. The image of Mikah looking down at me when I woke up from fainting yesterday pops back into my mind, and the urge to see him grows stronger. I look up to see what floor we're on. Forty-one. Almost there.

Ugh. It's stupid of me to want to see him again. He's everything I'm not, and I have no business thinking about him that way.

"When was the last time you ate?" a male voice says from behind me.

SIX

I jump, stop breathing and then try to sink further into the wall.

Without turning to look at him I mumble, "Uh, last night, with you."

Suddenly an arm reaches out for the panel in front of me. He presses stop and then presses the button with a phone on it.

A disembodied voice comes on the line. "Yes, sir?"

"Redirect us to the skyway level, please."

I huff.

"Yes, sir."

There are a couple of clicks, and the elevator starts to descend again. I'm still not looking at him.

"Why? What is so damn important about feeding me?" I try to growl and sound irritated, but the mention of food has made me hungry. Then again, I'm almost always hungry. But there's no way I'm accepting more charity from him. In fact, this is the perfect opportunity to give him his money back. Then I can leave via the skyway system and grab a bus back toward my apartment. It'll give me time to eat a hot dog, since it's still hours before I have to be at work.

"It's important to me because eating is healthy, and I don't like the way you look."

"Gah!" I exclaim. "Are you kidding me? What difference does it make to you what I look like? You're some random customer who's come into my diner for the last couple of nights. So what if I'm a little thin. That's my business and none of yours."

I look up, trying to see how long until we reach skyway level. I'm eager to get out of this conversation. We are still only in the upper twenties, and the skyway is on level two or three. Damn it.

I hear him sigh in frustration. "Because people, especially you, should not go without food."

Me? "What is so damn special about me?" I ask aloud. "For all you know I'm some random drug addict—"

"I know that's not the case," he says, cutting me off.

I finally look at him. His hair is slicked back in the same way it's been the other times I've seen him. His eyes are blue and warm, and there is a half smile playing at his lips. He's looking down at me, making me feel small at five feet, two inches. He has to be at least six feet tall. Broad shoulders. His suit today is gunmetal gray with blue or black pinstripes — I can't tell which. His shirt is a beautiful lavender color with a darker purple tie.

"How do you know I'm not an addict?" I ask softly.

He smiles at me, warm, genuine. "Because you've come to return the tip money I left you last night."

My jaw falls open. "How" — I swallow hard — "did you know?"

His smile fades a little. "Why else would you come down here?"

I close my mouth and look down at the floor. He says it almost as if my being here is unwelcome, but he has a point and his ability to read me is really scary.

"Since you haven't eaten since last night, I'm going to take you to lunch."

I feel my face flush bright red, both in anger and complete irritation. "That is not why I'm here. I've survived my entire life fending for myself, I don't need some rich, hot-shot businessman buying me food."

I reach into the pocket of my bag and pull the folded-up paper from it. I thrust it toward him. He refuses to take it. Tears of frustration trickle down my cheeks. "Damn it, Mikah, take it." I push it at him again, and again he refuses. "I'm not a damn charity case. I don't need your money or your food."

The bell chimes. We've finally reached the skyway. As soon as the doors open, I drop the folded-up paper with his money in it, bolt from the elevator and turn left, hoping and praying I can get away.

"Vivienne, stop," I hear him say behind me. I keep going, walking quickly but not running. Yet. I'm trying hard to not make a scene.

But he doesn't seem to care about that. He catches me quickly. Spins me around. I grab hold of his arm so I don't go sprawling onto the floor.

My stomach, on the other hand, has its own agenda. I cover my mouth quickly as my eyes dart around, looking for a restroom or at the very least a trashcan. I spot a trashcan about ten feet away.

I try in vain to free myself from his grip. "Damn it!" I bark at him. "I'm goin—" I swallow back the bile that's rising up my throat. "Throw up," I whisper. His grip immediately loosens on my arms and I dart to the trashcan.

He's there in an instant, pulling back my hair so that I don't vomit on it. Due to the empty state of my stomach, it doesn't last long, and I slink to the floor against the wall, drained and exhausted. Resting my head against the wall, I close my eyes. I feel a cool hand against my cheek and I flinch. A completely involuntary reaction.

"You should really go to the hospital," he says quietly as he pulls his hand back.

"For what? Ain't nothing they can do."

"In less that twenty-four hours, I've watched you faint and now vomit into a trashcan. You need to go to the hospital."

Oh for fuck's sake. "Damn it, Mikah, no. I don't need to go to the hospital. I'm pregnant, not diseased."

A harsh growl comes from between his lips. Thank God. Nothing scares a man away like the words *I'm pregnant.* I stand up, ready to try to leave again, knowing full well that he won't follow me this time.

I catch one last glimpse of his beautiful face. "Goodbye, Mikah," I say and take a step away from him.

SEVEN

I'm finally able to make it to the skyway and cross over to the next building. I follow the signs to an elevator and push the down button. A few other people join me in waiting.

I hear Mikah's voice talking to someone. "She went this way. You can't miss her – she has bright red hair, long, down to the small of her back."

I sink down into the crowd a little bit. The people around me are very pointedly staring at me. It's obvious that they know he's talking about me.

"Damn it, Vivienne," I hear him say, farther away this time.

Finally the elevator arrives. I'm quick to jump in. The rest of the little crowd follows behind me and I push *G* for ground level. Please, let me get out of here and on the bus before he catches up to me.

It takes but a few moments before the doors are opening on the first floor. As soon as they do, I see Mikah across the lobby, frantically looking for me. I draw my hood up over my head, hoping it'll hide my red hair. But it's a pretty day outside, and the hood may draw more attention. Damn it. I look to my left and spy an exit. Phew – I can slide that way and avoid him.

I put my head down and start moving along swiftly. All of a sudden I hear a man shout, "Blake!" followed by a whistle and the snapping of fingers far too close to me. I speed up.

I'm almost to the exit when a hand wraps around my upper arm. The grip is hard, painful. As he spins me around my hand comes up reflexively, hard and fast, and connects with his cheek.

"Shit!" he spats as his head snaps to the left with the impact of my hand. "Damn it, Viv, don't fight me."

"Jesus, Mikah, I'm—I didn—" I can feel the tears welling up in my eyes as I watch him rub his cheek. Regret fires through my heart as I realize that coming here was a really bad mistake. The tears spill over and I try to pull away from him.

"Hey, it's alright. I took you by surprise." He pulls me back toward him and wraps his arms around me.

I come completely unglued. Tears begin streaming, hot and heavy, down my cheeks as he cups me against his chest. Embarrassed by my lack of self-control, I push against him, trying to pull myself out of his arms.

"Vivienne, please, it's alright. Don't run."

The tears come even harder, stealing what little strength I had to begin with, and my legs begin to shake.

I give in to his embrace. It's strangely comforting being in his arms. I feel safe and protected, like nothing I've ever felt before.

With his hand over my left ear and my right pressed tight against him, I can't make out what he's saying, but I can feel the vibrations of his voice. He lifts his hand and says very gently, "I'm going to pick you up."

"No...no, no, no," I whine, but my protest is weak, and he ignores me. Sweeping me up off my feet, he walks through the doors I had been trying to get out of and onto the street. "Please, put me down."

"Not a chance, sweetheart. Not a chance." He shakes his head. "Not until we're in the car."

"Car? What car? No. Mikah, stop. I have to go to work." My protest falls upon deaf ears. I hear a car door open, and Mikah gracefully slides in. It's not until I'm inside that I realize that we're in a limousine. I want to protest more, but I know full well I'm going to lose the argument.

Then panic sets in. I don't like being locked into such a tight space. My body starts to shake again, harder than before, as my panic level rises.

"Hey." He pulls back to look at me. "Vivienne, what's the matter?"

I slip out of his grasp and crawl down onto the floor of the car. My teeth chatter, I'm shaking so bad. "T-t-tight...s-space. Claustro...ph-ph-phobic. Too...dark," I finally manage to say as images of the hot dark closet I'd spent several days in swirl inside my mind.

"Red, hit the lights and windows."

"Yes, sir."

Suddenly light floods into the limo and I can feel a cool breeze flowing in from outside. The shakes reduce to a slight tremor.

Mikah leans forward on the bench seat, almost as if he is going to join me on the floor. He reaches out for my arm and I flinch away at the contact. He hesitates momentarily then tries again. This time I don't flinch, and he begins to gently rub my arm. I find myself soothed by the caress.

"Why are we in a car? Where are we going?" I finally manage to ask.

"We're in the car because I want some privacy with you. We'll stay here until you're ready to go. Then I'm taking you to H.C.M.C."

I stiffen and pull away from his hand. I slide back against the bench opposite him and pull my knees to my chin, steeling myself.

"No. I told you, no hospital."

He reaches out toward me, but I shy away and he stops. "I just need to know that you're alright. Okay?" He looks down at me. His eyes are comforting, warm. "Please, Vivienne?" His voice is pleading, but not insistent. A hint of desperation.

My heart starts to pound and my skin tingles. I look away from his face, not wanting to see his reaction to what I'm about to tell him. I know what I will see and I can't stand the sight of pity in someone's eyes when they look at me. But he has to know why taking me to the hospital wouldn't help me.

"If I go to the hospital, I will lose my job because Bartie is an ass-hat and he won't care where I am. I'm malnourished. My blood sugar is low, and I have high levels of anxiety. There, sir, is your diagnosis. And you know what they will do? They will run a battery of tests on me that I can't afford just to tell me everything I've just told you. Then they'll tell me that I'm not taking proper care of myself. That I should eat regularly and get plenty of rest, which are completely unreasonable expectations given my circumstances. They will make me feel shitty and useless. Then they will send me home to a closet-sized apartment with no food, a half-ass thing the landlord calls a mattress, and no way to pay my rent or buy what little food I have been able to afford because I will be without a job. So what's the point?"

I don't need to look at him to be able to gage his reaction. "Mikah, I work shit hours at a shit job for shit pay. I live in an overly shitty apartment and have no means of changing that fact anytime soon. So this is me, who I am.

You're just going to have to deal with the fact that you can't save me." I start crying again, completely out of control.

"Jesus, Vivienne, why won't you let me help you?" His voice is soft, sincere and - more than anything - sad.

"Because! You have more important things to do than worry about some poor, pathetic, pregnant chick who works at a diner you stumbled into the other night. I've already told you — I've made it on my own, I will continue to make it on my own. Just like I always have. Please, Mikah.... Please respect that," I plead with him.

"I...Vivienne, I can't. I respect you for everything you've done, but you need more than you can provide for yourself. It's not just you that you need to worry about. I want to help you. And your baby." He takes a long, deep breath.

Guilt floods through me as I take in his words. "If I go to the hospital, get checked out, will that be enough for you? Will you walk away when I'm done?" I plead.

"I can't promise that."

"Damn it, why not? Mikah, you don't even know me."

"Vivienne Alison Callahan. Born September second, nineteen ninety, Boston Hospital. Born to mother Rebecca Callahan, father unknown."

I lift myself up onto the leather seat of the bench I've been leaning against to put as much distance between us as I can manage.

"Do you want me to continue?"

I shake my head. "Just because you know those facts does not mean you know me or who I am." Good God, he went digging for my history. Why would he do something like that? "You've known me less than three days. How on earth were you able to find that out?"

"I'm not sure you really want me to answer that." I glare at him. "When you flinched away from me after you fainted, I took off because...because..." He looks away from me. "Because I was afraid we would end up in this situation. In a car, heading to the hospital, with you feeling as though I'd trapped you in here."

My heart clenches tight.

"Please, Vivienne. Do this for me? There are reasons that I can't explain. It's not pity or charity. It's..." He pauses and looks back toward me. His eyes are warm, sincere. "It's a need that I don't understand. So please, let me help you."

"I..." I take a long, ragged breath.

"I understand your pride, your determination. Hell, I even admire it. But don't you think it's time you deserve a break? You deserve a chance to step back and take a break. Please, Vivienne, let me help you."

"Alright. I'll go," I say. I feel exhausted, emotionally drained. I barely register the fact that the car is in motion, but we're moving.

I realize deep down that he's right. I need to get checked out — at least for the baby's sake, if not my own — and honestly this might be the only way.

EIGHT

I'm brought out of my reverie when I hear Mikah shift in his seat. I look out the window and see the hospital as we pull into the parking lot. He leans forward and grabs my hand. This time I don't flinch away from him; I let his fingers slide in between mine.

"Come on. Let's go have you checked out." He smiles at me as the car comes to a stop. Tiny crinkles appear at the corners of his eyes, and I can tell that the smile is genuine.

"So can I say now that hospitals terrify me?"

His door opens and he starts to climb out. "Yes, you can tell me. But one of the biggest differences between your other trips here and this one is that you're not alone."

I can't believe I've agreed to let him take care of me. I'm not entirely sure what this is all going to imply, and it scares the hell out of me. I've taken care of myself since I was about six and my mother could no longer care for me.

When we enter, Mikah walks straight up to the nurse at the emergency care registration desk. "Mr. Blake. What can we do for you today?"

My heart sinks. They know him? How many other girls has he brought here?

"It's not me. Ms. Callahan is in need of some medical attention. She fainted last night." I roll my eyes. "Can we have her checked out?"

"Certainly. Ms. Callahan, why don't you follow me?" I look at Mikah, who is smiling reassuringly at me. I glare at him.

"What?" he mouths.

"Have you done this before?" I hiss.

"Done what? Come to this hospital?"

"Brought some lonely, practically homeless chick here?"

The shock that crosses his face tells me that I've said something offensive to him. "No, Vivienne, I don't go around preying on fainting, helpless women. I am the majority shareholder of this hospital."

My jaw clenches. Oh. But my pride won't let my anger fade so easily. "I'm sorry," I say, looking stonily into his eyes.

"You know, for being as small as you are, you put up one hell of a fight." He laughs a little. "Come on." He tugs at my hand, pulling me toward the nurse.

Twenty minutes later, I'm tucked into a room and getting into an open-back hospital gown. The cold material touching me makes me realize that I'm super sensitive, a live-wire. It reminds me of getting sick, when my skin is achy from catching a cold.

I lie back against the cold mattress and pull the blankets up to my armpits as Mikah enters. Suddenly I'm exhausted. My eyes feel like sandbags. Mikah takes a seat in the chair next to the bed, and I slowly close my eyes.

I wake up a few minutes later to the sound of Mikah's voice. He's talking to someone. "She fainted last night after eating a meal. Something I'm guessing she hasn't done in some time."

"Why not?" A female voice. "On purpose?"

"No, no. Nothing like that."

"Okay. Well, we will do some blood work. And I recommend an ultrasound. You know this isn't the first time she's been in here, right?"

Oh, no. I stir in the bed and open my eyes.

"Hi, Vivienne. I'm Dr. Alston." She extends her hand to me.

I try to sit up, but I'm weak with exhaustion. Suddenly there's a whirring noise and the top half of the bed starts to rise.

"Thanks," I mutter in Mikah's direction.

Then I notice a tugging underneath my gown. I look down at the wires coming out at the neckline. My eyes follow them towards the vitals monitor to my left. Turning my head back towards the doctor I notice the clip on my finger.

I extend my hand to Dr. Alston. "We've met before," I say, hoping Mikah doesn't ask too many questions.

"Pleasure to see you again. Mikah tells me you fainted yesterday after eating?" I nod. "Can you describe for me how you felt right before?"

"I was irritated," I said, darting a glance at Mikah. "Then I stood, the room spun and I realized that I was falling. The next thing I remember was waking up on the floor."

"Any headache after you fainted?" I shake my head. "Have you been dizzy since then?" I shake my head. "What about vomiting?"

"Twice."

"When?" She's looking from me to Mikah and I don't understand why.

"Once this morning, as soon as I woke up. Then again about an hour ago." I don't feel the need to add that a nightmare about that abusive asshole of an ex-boyfriend was the reason for my vomiting.

"I spun her around this morning, before I found out she was pregnant, and she vomited into a trashcan in the skyway downtown."

The doctor just nods and writes something else in her notepad.

"I throw up nearly every morning," I add.

"Do you remember about how far along you are?" I shake my head. I've tried to forget everything related to the last time I was here. "Okay, here's what we're going to do. I want to draw some blood and start an IV." My stomach churns at the thought of not one but two needles. "We need to get some fluids and some vitamins in you. Okay?"

I shake my head. "I don't like needles."

"I understand, but it is the fastest, best way to get you rehydrated. I can tell from the bluish veins in your arm that you're very dehydrated. You're also very malnourished. We need to check your blood sugar and run a few other tests. I also want to have an ultrasound done. This way we can take a good look at what stage in the pregnancy you are." She gestures to my stomach. "Can I take a look first?"

"Does he have to stay?" I ask, nodding in Mikah's direction. Some things are better done in private.

"I just want to do an external examination, but if you want him to leave..." She looks pointedly at Mikah.

"Vivienne, if it's okay, I'd like to stay." His hand lightly strokes the back of mine. I flinch at the unexpected contact. I look at Dr. Alston.

"Mikah, why don't you give us a few moments alone," she says. "When I'm done you can come right back in here. Okay?" Mikah shoots a glance at me, then looks back to the doctor.

"It's okay," I tell him. "I'll let you back in."

He nods, his face somber as he stands and exits the room.

Dr. Alston closes the door behind him. Turning to me, she says, "Are you okay?"

I try to nod, but it's slow and small. The look on Mikah's face as I asked him to leave has me wondering what he's thinking, why he is so upset.

"I saw you flinch. Is Mikah the reason you were here two months ago?"

I'm shocked by the suggestion that Mikah could do that to me, but then I realize that she really has no way of knowing who put me here the last time. "No. I only met him a couple days ago. At the diner I work at. He bought me dinner last night, then tried to leave me a five hundred dollar tip and his business card. I went to his office today to give it back to him. I threw up, and he dragged me here."

"You don't want to be here?"

I shake my head.

"Why not?"

"I hate hospitals. The last time I was here, I spent three days here. I can't afford that kind of time, let alone the cost. I'm supposed to be to work at four."

"Mr. Blake has already informed billing that he is paying for everything today. In fact, for all your future visits here."

"What?" When the hell did he manage that? Irritation races through me and the machine beeps frantically as my heart rate increases.

"Calm down, Vivienne. He's a good person with a good heart. Maybe you should ask him why this is so important to him. You might better understand."

"I've tried." I look down at the sheet. I can hear the monitor slow as my heart rate calms.

"Give him some time. He'll come around. It is my duty as a doctor to make sure that Mikah is not the reason you flinched and that no harm has come to you by his hand, but my guess is that it has more to do with why you were here the last time." I nod, unable to look at her. "I don't want to pry, but we can set you up with someone to talk to."

I shake my head. "I appreciate that, but I'm alright." Sitting down and talking to a shrink creeps me out. When I was here the last time, they made one of the shrinks on staff come talk to me. He was a jerk and didn't seem to really care. He kept looking at his phone each time it buzzed. They let me go the next day, so obviously my silence didn't make him think I was nuts.

She shrugs her shoulders. No doubt she doesn't believe that I'm okay. She is probably right.

"How about you let me take a look?" She gestures again to my belly.

"Can Mikah come back in?" I ask before I can stop myself. If he's in here, she won't ask me any more questions about Riley.

"Of course," she says as she goes to the door to open it.

Mikah is right there.

"Come on in, Mikah."

His eyes dart from her to me and back again. I don't understand why he's so nervous.

"She said you can come back in," Dr. Alston tells him. "I was just about to start the examination."

His eyes widen.

"It's alright, come in," I say to him.

He nods and comes back into the room, taking the same seat as before.

I reach my hand out toward him, and he smiles a little. Something about his touch calms me.

The second our hands make a connection, my heart beats three times really fast. Okay, maybe *calms* is the wrong word.

We lock gazes. He lifts one eyebrow, then, as if to experiment, he pulls his hand away. My heart rate slows way down for a couple of beats before resuming a normal rhythm.

"What in the world?" I hear Dr. Alston say.

I look at Mikah. He's smiling like a Cheshire cat.

"Watch," he says.

Once the doctor's attention is fixed on us, he reaches for my hand again. Again my heart beats three times in rapid succession. Then he pulls his hand away, and my heart misses a beat, speeds up for a few seconds and then goes back to normal. Next to me, Mikah chuckles, causing me to smile.

"That is the strangest, most bizarre thing I've ever seen," Dr. Alston says, looking at me. "Well then, shall we?" She pulls on a pair of examination gloves.

I nod, but my heart rate increases again. I want her to turn it off so my emotions aren't so obvious, but at the same time I find strange comfort in being able to hear the reaction my heart has to him. I suddenly wish Mikah was attached to it, too. I'm curious whether I have the same effect on him.

"I'm going to keep you covered, but I need to lift your gown." I nod as Mikah lays the bed back down. "That's good," Dr. Alston says, and the bed comes to a stop.

I can still see everything she is doing. She pulls the blanket down and then gently slides it under my gown to cover my pubic area. Once the blanket is in place, she lifts the gown, bringing it to rest just under my breasts. Next to me, Mikah gasps.

"When was your last period, Vivienne?" the doctor asks, completely calm.

"Um, I don't know. Late June or early July. I discovered in August I was pregnant. The morning before I was here last."

Mikah's hand tightens against mine and his body goes rigid. He is no doubt contemplating the significance of that last statement.

"Okay, and if I remember correctly, you were four or five weeks along then. So that will put you between eleven and thirteen weeks." Her hands on my belly are cold; my stomach flinches at her touch. "Sorry," she says quickly.

I look down my body at my stomach. There are three very visible, well-defined points: Each of my hipbones are sharp against my skin, and the ominous bump from yesterday looks bigger from this angle. No wonder that skirt felt tight this morning. I hadn't worn it since my interview at the diner almost two months ago.

She pokes and pushes, doing what doctors do, and I flinch when some of the pressure points cause me pain.

"You're very skinny. Have you always been this way?"

I hesitate to answer her. The answer is no, I haven't. In fact, I used to be about a size ten or twelve, but I'm not sure I really want to highlight the fact that I've lost a lot of weight in the last six or seven months. The direct result of being told by Riley that I was fat — just one of the ways he had of bringing me down — and then of not being able to afford to buy food. After I left the hospital, it became increasingly difficult to take care of myself.

I shake my head. "No, not always." I have no doubt that Dr. Alston is pissed off at me for not taking better care of myself. Believe me, if I could afford more food, I'd eat it. It's not like I'm not trying.

She gently pulls the gown back down. "Aside from your weight — which is a big issue — everything looks okay. I'll have the nurse come in and get your IV and blood work going. I'll put in for an ultrasound, and I will be back in a little while." She pulls off the gloves and starts washing her hands in the sink. "Can I get you anything?" she asks, reaching for the paper towels.

"Another blanket would be good." I'm freezing again.

"I'll send one in. There is a button on the side of your bed if you need anything else."

"What about some food?" Mikah asks her.

Dr. Alston nods. "Keep it light, though. Soup or pudding would be good."

"Thanks, doctor." He looks at me. "Are you hungry?"

I start to shake my head and he scowls at me. It's actually pretty cute.

"Fine, yes, I'll eat." I smile at him and his eyes light up. His answering smile is blinding. "Why does that make you so happy?" I ask.

"Because you deserve far better than you're giving yourself, and I'm happy to give it. Whenever and however I can." I feel his hand tighten around mine. "Thank you."

He's thanking *me*? "What for?"

"For coming in, talking to the doctor. Being so calm about this and..." He pauses, looking deep into my eyes.

Something happens between us in this moment, a shift of some sort that I don't understand, and the heart monitor broadcasts my fluttering heartbeat. Geez, that is so embarrassing.

He smiles again. "And for letting me be here with you. Speaking of which, why did she make me leave only to have me come back in?" I look down from his penetrating blue-green eyes. "Tell me," he pleads.

"She saw me flinch when you touched my hand. She was concerned that you were the reason I was here the last time."

His face grows pale, and I feel his whole body go cold as he realizes why I was here a couple of months ago.

"I told him I was pregnant and he didn't like that very much. He took it out on me," I whisper.

"Fuck!" he spats, and I can feel his body start to tremble.

I can't look at him. I'm so ashamed. Ashamed of the fact that I was beaten, that Riley beat me whenever he felt like it. Ashamed that I let it happen more than once. I start to cry.

"I'm going to touch your head," Mikah says, finally getting why I flinch every time he touches me unexpectedly. "I want to..."

But I don't want his comforting. I feel the anger radiating from him, and though I know it's not directed at me, my broken spirit is already trying to push him away, to undo the intimacy between us. "It's okay. I'm okay," I sob.

"Like hell you are. I'm not going to hurt you or hit you. I would never – *will* never do anything to harm you. Ever." His voice is full of conviction.

I squeeze my eyes tight against the tears, willing them to stop, but I can't seem to control them. Then I feel his hand resting lightly against the top of my head. So light that I almost can't feel it. Then slowly, steadily, he starts to caress my head, stroking my hair. The movement is methodical, but it doesn't feel empty. My scalp tingles as goose bumps rise across it, then my neck, down my back and across my arms. My heart beats faster, keeping the machine busy with each pump and flutter.

He shifts closer to me. Keeping our hands entwined, he puts his head down on the pillow next to mine. "Please don't cry," he says quietly. His breath warms my cheek.

My heart continues to flutter, and a warm tingling sensation runs through my body, wrapping me in a feeling of comfort, safety, and an inexplicable need for his touch.

"Please, don't stop," I say softly.

"Never."

NINE

I wake up to a nurse coming in with a whole lot of stuff. Something that looks like a T.V. and a tray filled with vials.

"Hi, Vivienne. I'm Amanda. I'll be your nurse. I'm here to take your blood and get you set up with an IV. Once that's done, we will get you ready for your ultrasound. How are you feeling?"

"Tired," I groan. When I cry, it drains me completely and I just want to sleep. I think it is more of an escape-from-reality kind of thing than a physical need for sleep.

Mikah laughs. "She was sleeping when you came in," he says from much closer to my head than I expected. He's still stroking my hair, and his other thumb is rubbing along the back of my hand.

"Good. Sorry I woke you."

"It's okay."

I watch as she sets her tray of vials down on the table and starts going in for what she needs. As soon as she pulls out a tourniquet I roll toward Mikah, not wanting to see what she's about to do.

"I understand you're not a fan of needles. I'm going to do my best to not hurt you. I've been told I'm pretty good at being gentle." I nod. "Left arm, I take it?"

I nod again and she lifts my left arm, pulling it back slightly so it's out of my line of sight.

"Look at me," Mikah says.

I lift my chin upwards and find his piercing green eyes on me. That's strange; earlier they were more of a blue-green, but now they're almost completely green. Emerald. Almost like he put contacts in while I was sleeping.

The monitor sputters again. He smiles wide, and Nurse Fang — as I'm calling her in my head — has the tourniquet around my arm. I flinch as the needle pierces my skin.

"Long. Deep. Breath." I do as Mikah says and inhale slowly.

While it doesn't hurt, I can feel her shifting the needle around for nearly a whole minute before she hits pay dirt and releases the tourniquet from my arm.

She fills four vials with my blood; I feel a slight tug as each vial is replaced with the next one. Then the needle moves around again as she gets the IV set up. The tape comes next, and before I know it she's done. I let out the breath I was holding and Mikah smiles at me.

"Wow. Very well done, Vivienne," Nurse Fang — *Amanda,* I remind myself — says approvingly.

"Thanks. You're not so bad yourself."

She laughs. "I do try as best as I can. Can you roll back onto your back for me?" I shake my head in protest. "Please?" she pleads. She sounds almost like a whiny teenager and I roll my eyes.

"I'm comfortable."

"I know, but I'm going to get you set up for your ultrasound and the tech will be in here very shortly."

I sigh and reluctantly roll over. I realize I'm putting up a bigger fight than what I really feel.

Amanda repeats the procedure of pulling the blanket up to cover my pubis and raising the gown to reveal the little round mound between my hips. I hear Mikah's sharp intake of breath as my belly is exposed again. I can't tell if he's in awe or if it's a tortured sound. For my part, I'm starting to see that the mound and what it represents is unavoidable. Surprisingly, it's also growing more adorable each time I see it.

Amanda finishes up and leaves.

I look at Mikah. "Are you okay?" I ask him. He nods. "Is it hard for you to look at me like this?"

"Yes." He hears my heart skip a beat. "Not in the way you're thinking," he adds quickly. I give him a puzzled look, but he just shakes his head. "I will explain it to you later. Okay?" he asks, his voice soft.

I nod, still confused but trusting he will tell me later. I look up at the clock and panic sets in. It's three thirty and I'm supposed to be at work in half an hour. Stupid heart monitor goes nuts, and Mikah stands and leans into my line of sight.

"What's the matter?" he says, worried.

"I'm supposed to be at the diner in thirty minutes. I can't lose this job." Panic creeps into my voice.

"It's already been arranged. I spoke with Laura while you were sleeping, and she said that she would deal with Bartie and to keep her posted. If you were going to be gone longer than Sunday's shift we might have a problem, but right now, one day is okay. She said that she was going to tell him that you and Nyssa switched places because of Tuesday night?" The question in his voice tells me he's relaying a message he doesn't quite understand.

I take a deep breath and let it out slowly. "Thank you," I say quietly. "I do hope you're right. I can't afford to lose that job."

"Yes, you can." Or at least I think that's what he said. He was mumbling incoherently.

"What?" I scowl at him.

"Later."

"Why all this 'later' crap with you?" I huff.

"Because the doctor is coming in." And sure enough there is a knock on the door. How the hell did he know that? I leave the question for later and instead roll my eyes.

"How're you feeling?" Dr. Alston asks.

"Okay, just sleepy." She nods and walks over to the machine Amanda brought in, clicks a few buttons, and the screen flickers to life.

"I'm going to go ahead and handle your ultrasound," she says gently. Then she presses a couple of keys on a keyboard that came with the monitor and grabs a white bottle that looks a lot like the ketchup bottles at the diner, but with a shorter nozzle. I can't tell what's actually in the bottle.

"This might feel a little cold," she says right before the substance hits my belly. I watch as my belly flinches at the clear gel being squirted on it. "Now I'm going to use this." She holds a wand type thing that is wide and flat at the top. "I'm going to place it against your stomach and see what we can see. Okay?"

I nod. My heart starts pounding; it sounds super loud on the machine. Dr. Alston reaches over and presses a couple of buttons on the heart monitor. The beep gets quieter.

Mikah, who has been very quiet in the corner, gently squeezes my hand. I look over at him. His eyes are not on the doctor or the monitor; they are on me, on my face. I smile at him nervously and he squeezes my hand again as Dr. Alston presses the wand against my abdomen.

TEN

"Well, well. Hello there, little one," Dr. Alston croons.

I pull my eyes from Mikah's to look at the doctor, who is very intently looking at the monitor. The angle I'm at makes the monitor look black, and I can't see anything. The wand moves around on my stomach while Dr. Alston presses various buttons on the machine.

"Can we see?" I ask quietly.

As soon as the words leave my mouth, I have a sudden rush of fear. I want to see, but I'm scared. I'm scared that seeing the baby will make it real for me.

Mikah squeezes my hand again as Dr. Alston presses a couple more buttons.

"Just a...moment. I'm taking measurements. This will help us determine the age of the fetus, along with your blood work."

I bite my lip nervously and Mikah's hand resumes stroking my hair. This time, although I wasn't expecting his touch, I don't flinch, and I'm suddenly very grateful that she's turned down the heart monitor. His touch sends invisible shivers across my body, and I feel the knot in my stomach loosening.

That's when I realize that the knot has been in my stomach for months, not just minutes.

With a couple more clicks of the keys, she grabs the side of the monitor to turn it. Panic sets in and my heart rate skyrockets.

"Calm down, Vivienne. It's okay. I can give you some pictures instead, so you can look at them when you're ready."

I pull in a few long breaths, trying to imagine what this is going to be like, how I'm going to react. I remind myself that I chose this, that this is what I want.

"No." I take another long, deep breath. "I'm ready," I say, and once again, Mikah's silent reassurance is there as he squeezes my hand.

Dr. Alston slowly turns the monitor until the image comes into view.

It's grainy, black and white, narrow at the top and wider at the bottom. Smack in the middle of the screen is a black, odd-shaped oval, and inside that oval is...

Tears, hot and heavy, flow down my cheeks. There are no words for the beautiful image I see on the screen. Two arms, two legs, a head all visible. Suddenly the image zooms in, and I can see the baby's profile: faintest outline of eyes, nose, a faint shadow of lips.

"My God," Mikah says, so softly I almost miss it. Reverence in his voice. Part of me wants to see the expression on his face, but I can't pull my eyes away from the monitor.

To the right of a wedge shape on the monitor, something is pulsing. I point toward it with my free hand. "What. Is. That?"

"A strong heartbeat. Want to hear it?" Dr. Alston asks. I nod and she reaches for something on the keyboard. A second pulse enters the room.

"It's so fast," I say as I watch the pulsing match up with the noise. It almost sounds like a bad radio signal, full of static, but it is the sweetest sound I've ever heard. I start to cry again.

"That's very normal at this stage of pregnancy. In fact, up until well after delivery. Babies' heart rates run faster than ours for a while.

"As I suspected, you're about eleven to twelve weeks along. The baby is measuring at about three inches in length. In another five or six weeks, we should be able to fully determine the sex."

"When you say 'fully determine'...?" Mikah asks her.

"I mean that I can take a guess right now, based off of what I saw, but it would be a guess of experience and not expertise. Do you want to know what I think it is, Vivienne?"

I shake my head, wiping tears from my eyes. "I would rather wait until you're sure." My voice comes out hardly above a whisper.

She smiles at me and says, "That sounds like a plan to me. Do you want to take some pictures with you?" I nod and lay my head back against the pillow. I'm still tired but feeling a little bit stronger. I'm guessing it's the fluids being pumped into me.

Dr. Alston has frozen the monitor and pulled the wand away. On the screen is a still image of my baby's profile. It has to be the most beautiful thing I've ever seen. She pushes a few buttons again and I can hear a machine start up below me. Then she leans down and hands me a stack of several pictures, all black and white. Fuzzy, but still beautiful.

I feel the bed start to rise and I look at Mikah. His eyes are slightly red. Tears? That would explain why he was so quiet...but why? Why would he be crying over my baby? Then again, I can't imagine how Dr. Alston does this without crying. It really is a beauty of life.

"Okay," Dr. Alston interrupts my thoughts. "I'm going to go and see if your blood work is back, check on a couple of things and then we can decide on a plan of action." She releases the brake on the ultrasound cart with her foot and begins to pull it out the door.

I turn toward Mikah, and he beats me to my question. "How are you doing?" he asks. His raspy voice sends goose bumps across my skin.

"I'm scared."

"Of?" he asks.

"Everything. I don't know. But seeing that...just..." I pause, blinking back the tears again. "It just brings it all into reality."

He doesn't say anything for a long time. I rest my head back against the bed and close my eyes, but all I can see is that little baby. My baby. Until a few minutes ago, the life growing inside me didn't have much impact on my everyday life, but now, reality is setting in and I can't even begin to imagine how I'm going to do this. I'm an only child. I had friends growing up, but never really a baby around to take care of. I started to babysit when I was twelve or so, but those were usually kids just a couple years younger than I was.

Wanting to see the baby again, I open my eyes and look down at the pictures in my hand. In the upper left-hand corner it has my name, and in the upper right-hand corner it says *Baby Callahan.*

A sense of relief washes over me, seeing that and not Riley's last name. Then I feel the disappointment as I realize that, just like me, there will be no father's name on my baby's birth certificate.

"Vivienne?"

"Hmm?" I say, looking up from the picture and into Mikah's eyes. They are soft, warm, and a beautiful green.

"I'm wondering now if you will let me help you?"

"You already are. You're paying for this hospital visit and any other visits I need to make here."

"You know?"

I nod. "And...I appreciate it. Thank you, Mikah."

His lips curl at the corners slightly, like he's fighting a smile. "That's not what I'm referring to," he says.

"No, Mikah. While I appreciate your willingness to pay for my medical expenses, I have to do the rest on my own." I'm only accepting his help with the hospital bills because I can now see it's a necessity, but I draw the line at letting him help me with other things. What would he expect in return? Nothing I'd want to give, surely.

"How, Vivienne? How on earth do you plan to do this on your own? You can't even afford to feed yourself, let alone that beautiful baby."

My heart flutters at his words, which make me feel weak and unable to take care of myself. So many things start flying through my head about my past. Mom's boyfriends calling her useless, then Riley making me feel as though I couldn't make it without him. I'm trying so hard to leave those ideas behind.

"I will get a second job. I'll go back to the shelter. I don't know, Mikah, but this is not your responsibility. It is mine."

"Damn it, Vivienne, please don't be so stubborn. I just want to help you."

"Mikah, we've had this conversation already. I will find a way on my own. I'm capable of it, I've done it for years."

"Don't give me that bullshit, Vivienne, you are skin and bones."

All the years of not fighting back pour into what comes out of my mouth. "Stop it, please, just stop. You make me feel like a complete imbecile when you say shit like that. I'm not stupid, despite what you think about my job, and I'm smarter than I look. Just because I don't have some Ivy League education doesn't mean I'm not capable of taking care of myself. I will not be treated like this by you or anyone else." Fury races through my body. "Forcing me to take your help – demanding that I bow down like some servant at your feet while I gulp up all the help you can offer – will get you nowhere with me. If you want to help me, Mikah, forget about me. Go back to the life you had twenty-four hours ago. I'm not worth it."

The tears flow harder, faster, and I break out into full-on sobs. I pull my hand from his and rub at my eyes, burying my face in my hands. He reaches up to take my hand, but I pull it away from him and turn to face the opposite direction.

"Vivienne?"

I don't answer him. I'm afraid my answer will just piss him off, and I don't want to know what the outcome of that will be.

"Vivienne. Please? I'm sorry," he pleads.

"Just get out," I say.

"No, I want to stay."

"Damn it, Mikah, get out of here! Go home, go back to work, go...wherever it is you feel you need to be."

"I need to be here, with you."

"No, you don't! Now get out before I call the nurse!"

I feel the air around him go cold. My body starts to shake as panic sets in. I've upset him, made him mad.

The bed jerks slightly as he pulls back from it. I hear him stand and walk to the door. The knob turns, the door clicks. A couple more steps and I hear the door swing closed behind him.

The sobs start immediately. What have I done?

Riley's voice comes back to me, blasting through my ears and my brain. *You're a no-good whore. You're good for nothing, you will always be nothing, and you deserve nothing.*

My whole body convulses with sobs. I can't stop. I can't breathe. I pull in quick breaths, on the verge of hyperventilation.

I can't. I can't do this. What was I thinking? I can't possibly do this on my own. All he wanted to do was help, and I pushed him away. For God's sake, he was red eyed after the ultrasound. He was here, holding my hand, stroking my hair, supporting me, being here for me, and I just threw him out of my room.

I really am hyperventilating now. I'm not getting enough air, and I can't seem to calm myself down. I manage to press the call button. A glance up at the monitor confirms that my heart rate is climbing. I hit the button again and again. Then suddenly I hear feet running in the hall, shouts coming from outside the door. I'm desperate for air. Just as the door flies open I vomit all over the bed and black out.

ELEVEN

I come to slowly, my eyes fluttering before opening, and the first thing that hits me is that I'm in a different room. This one's decorated in a soft pink, and the lights are dimmed. I hear paper shuffling to my left and I close my eyes again, tight, hoping it's not him.

"He's not here," a female voice says. Dr. Alston? "He left just before you lost consciousness. Said that you asked him to leave. Why?" I just shake my head. "He was quite upset when he left here."

"I asked him to leave because he sees me as a charity case."

"Sometimes our pride gets in the way of seeing the truth," she says softly. I open my eyes and look at her. She is sitting in a small recliner, a binder on her lap. She's wearing dark-framed glasses, and her platinum blond hair is no longer pulled back. Instead of scrubs, she's in a full-length black skirt and sequined blouse that shimmers in the soft light.

She notices me staring. "Sorry. I have a benefit event to go to in just a little while," she explains. "But I wanted to stay up here as long as I could. I was hoping you'd wake up. I wanted to talk to you about your blood work."

"Is everything alright?"

She nods. "Everything is okay under the circumstances. You're pregnant and undernourished. Your white blood cell count is low, and that means you're more susceptible to infections. But the good news is, you don't have any of the more serious conditions that usually cause white blood cell counts to be low, so I'm guessing that a healthier diet will boost that right back up. In the meantime, I've given you some vitamins through your IV that should help start the process. You need to finish it by eating and getting more sleep."

I try to nod, not sure how I'm going to manage what she is asking me to do.

"I've made a couple of phone calls for you. Have you ever heard of food stamps or W.I.C.?"

"No."

"Well, food stamps are part of a state-funded program that allows people and families with limited income to obtain food, and W.I.C. is a program available for children and pregnant woman. It provides food vouchers for additional things that you need."

"I never knew." How could I have not known all this time there was help available? Why was I not told about this at the shelter? Or why didn't Yvonne, my social worker, tell me?

"Well, now you do. There are also other programs out there that can help you. I've made an appointment for you for Monday morning with W.I.C. The details are in the pile of papers on the tray next to you, along with some more information about food stamps and W.I.C. In the meantime, H.C.M.C. is a county hospital, and we have a couple of programs that provide emergency assistance to patients. I've taken the liberty of arranging for some emergency food stamps and emergency cash. This will help get you home as well as get you some much-needed food. I can only lead you to it, though. You have to do the rest."

I nod. "Thank you."

"You need to take care of you. And that beautiful baby you're carrying." She closes the binder and stands up. "Believe me when I tell you, pride can be a royal pain in the ass. Sometimes you have to let it go."

"I'm trying, but it's hard."

"I know, and I understand. But think about this: If you can take what I've arranged for you, maybe you can consider whatever it is that Mikah's trying to offer you. I can almost guarantee there are no strings attached. He's not that kind of man."

I take a deep breath, trying to wash away all the thoughts of strings attached. "I will try," I say, quiet as a mouse. I'm tempted to explain to her my hesitation at accepting his help, but the wounds are deep and it would take more than one friendly conversation to want to share them.

She comes to sit at the foot of the bed, looking at me. "I've arranged for you to be discharged as soon as you're ready to go. On one condition?"

Oh great. "What condition?"

"That you stay at least until tomorrow morning. I'd like you to stay, get some dinner and eat some more in the morning. It's getting late and I know how difficult it would be to get something to eat where you live. So please, stay tonight. Have dinner, then breakfast, and whatever else you want in between now and then. Then go home. The nurse on duty in the morning can arrange a cab to come and pick you up. Or she can call Mr. Blake for you. Either way, get yourself to a store and buy some groceries. I've included a diet to help with the malnutrition and bring you back up to normal."

I try to remind myself that she is helping and not patronizing me or my abilities to take care of myself. "Thank you. For everything."

"It's my job," she states without any hint of irritation.

"Helping a girl like me medically is a part of your job, but not like this. So thank you."

"My pleasure, Vivienne." She turns to leave. "Oh" — spinning back around to look at me — "I almost forgot. As I am now your doctor, I've made an appointment for two weeks from today – Friday at nine forty-five – here at the hospital. I have a private practice space on the 3rd floor. I want to meet with you to see how things are going. After that, we will meet about every four weeks for regular ultrasounds. If you can't make an appointment, you need to call the number on my card. If anything happens and you can't get to me, call that card and I will come to you. Day or night."

Knowing that this is no doubt Mikah's doing actually pisses me off, and my face starts to turn red.

She reads my mind. "This is not his doing," she says. "It's mine, and on my dime. You need someone to help look after you, and there are so many programs out there to help pregnant girls just like you that most people don't know about. So please, if you come across a girl that needs help, send them here and have them ask for me by name. I will help them in any way I can."

I'm blown away by her generosity. Are there really people that good in the world?

And then I think that maybe Mikah, too, was just being generous. Maybe, just maybe, he really was trying to help without further motivation.

Tears prick. "Th-thank you," I stutter.

"You're most welcome. I mean it — anything, you call. Got it?"

"Yes, ma'am."

"Oh, and one last thing. If you don't call and don't show up to an appointment we have scheduled, I will call him. I have utter faith in his ability to track you down."

Oh, no! I'm pretty sure I make a face at her, but I get her point so I nod.

"Alright. Try and get some sleep tonight. You're safe here. And if I don't make it in before you're discharged, I will see you in two weeks."

"I will be here. Or I'll call."

"Good. See you then." And just like that, she's gone.

TWELVE

After Dr. Alston leaves, I start to go through the paperwork she left on the tray for me.

In the pile are several pamphlets about the various programs for women in my situation and a book, *What to Expect When You're Expecting*. There are also a few brochures on support groups for people processing past abuse, which I find strangely comforting. I'll have to try it out.

There is also an envelope that contains two hundred dollars in cash in various denominations. After what she told me earlier, I wouldn't have thought twice about it, except that the food stamp vouchers are in an official-looking envelope, and this isn't. Is this money out of her own pocket?

I'm trying very hard to accept the money without throwing a fit, regardless of its source. I have enough money in my— "Oh, No!" I exclaim, looking around frantically.

"'Oh no' what?" a female voice says from the door.

My head snaps up and I see Nurse Fang from the blood draw earlier.

"My stuff?"

"In here," she says, pointing to the closet door. "Did you need something?"

"My purse, please?"

"Sure." She opens the door and looks around. I can see my skirt and top hanging on the back of the door. After a moment she bends down and retrieves my purse. The panic I hadn't realized was building in me rushes away in a flash as she hands me my purse.

"Thanks."

"Of course. How are you feeling?"

"Much better." I suddenly realize that my bladder's uncomfortably full. "I need to go to the bathroom, actually."

"No problem. I'll show you how to unlock the IV pole so it will move with you. Then you can move around freely. After you eat, I want you to take a nice long walk around this wing. If you can handle that okay, I'll remove your IV. Sound like a plan?"

I nod, and she shows me the button on the IV pole that unlocks the wheels.

I climb gingerly out of bed, testing my feet to make sure I'm stable before I take a step. Upon entering the bathroom I'm grateful to see that the mirror isn't staring me in the face. I'm not sure I want to know what kind of messy state I'm in.

After only about a minute and a half, Amanda knocks. "You okay?"

I roll my eyes. "Yep."

When I come back out — still avoiding the mirror because I'm sure I'm hollowed out again — I climb back into bed and tell Amanda, "I'm ready to eat." It's been more than twenty-four hours since I ate last.

"I thought so. I ordered some soup, crackers and fresh fruit for you. You can have more whenever you want, but first I want to make sure it doesn't come right back up. Deal?"

I nod, slipping the white envelope with the money into my purse. Between this, what's left of my paycheck and the money Mikah foisted on me, I'll actually have some left after paying rent. Maybe with the little extra, I can find myself a new book at the used book store near the laundromat. A little something small for me?

"So are you babysitting me all night?" I ask as she's documenting my chart.

She laughs. "No, I'm just here until you eat, take a walk, and get settled in for the night. Is that okay?"

I snort. "Do I get a choice?"

She laughs again. "Nope, not really."

I chuckle. "At least that's settled." I smile. "Can I use this phone?" I ask, pointing to the phone beside the bed.

She nods. "The T.V., too."

"I don't watch T.V., but thank you." She gives me a puzzled look. "A luxury I can't afford," I explain. She nods and I dig into my bag for the little notebook I keep important information in, such as phone numbers.

As soon as I open it, Mikah's card falls out. I feel my chest tighten, and I quickly tuck it back out of sight. So far I've done a good job of holding myself in check and not thinking about him.

I find the number I'm looking for and dial. The phone rings three times, and then I'm met with a lot of noise. "Hello?"

"Hi, Laura, it's Vivienne."

"Oh my goodness. Hi, sweetheart. Are you okay?"

"Yeah, I'm fine. I'm staying in the hospital tonight."

"Oh dear."

"Don't worry, I will fill you in later. Was Bartie pissed?"

"Oh, sweetheart, no. I had Nyssa covering your shift before I told him. She said that she would cover Sunday for you as well."

"No need, but thank you. I'll be back in Sunday. Tell Nyssa I can cover her Tuesday shift, if she needs."

"I'll tell her, but she seemed pretty concerned when I called her today, so don't count on it. Okay?"

"Alright. I'll see you Sunday?" I say before she can start questioning me again.

"Okay, sweetheart."

"Thanks, Laura."

"Anytime. Bye, Viv."

"Bye." I hang up the phone.

I look to Amanda, who is smiling at me. "Is everything okay?"

I nod. "I work for a jerk of a boss that tends to be a bit on the harsh side if you don't work a scheduled shift. He's fired two girls since I've been there because they didn't show up, whether they called or not. So I wanted to make sure I still had a job."

"And?" she prompts.

"For now." I smile. "One of the girls covered my shift and offered to cover Sunday's as well."

"That might not be a bad idea. Get some extra rest."

"I wish I could, but I can't afford to go without the pay. Today will be hard enough to make up in tips. Which is why I offered to cover her Tuesday shift."

"I'm sure it will all work out," she says. She is trying to be nice, but I'm sure she has a hard time relating to being without money. The rock on her right ring finger is a dead giveaway.

There is a knock on the door. My heart stops. Before Amanda turns to open the door, she pauses to look at me reassuringly. She opens the door and I let out a rushed breath when I see it's a hospital staff member carrying a tray.

"Hi, Harold," Amanda says, opening the door wider so he can come in.

"Hi, Amanda. Ms. Callahan." He nods in my direction and I breathe in deeply through my nose. "Here you are, sweetheart. Have a nurse call if you'd like anything else," he says as he sets the tray down on the table and slides it in front of me. He pulls the dome off of the top, and the smell of chicken noodle soup fills my nose. It smells good.

"Thank you, Harold."

"Anytime." He smiles at me and quietly leaves the room.

"I'll let you eat. I'll be back in a little bit."

"Okay," I say. She follows Harold out the door, shutting it behind her.

Now that I'm alone with my thoughts and my dinner, I have a hard time moving past what happened with Mikah earlier today. He was only trying to be there for me, and I was being a bitch – something that he most certainly does not deserve. Slurping a spoonful of soup, I contemplate calling him and decide that all I would do is torture myself because I can't be the all-accepting person he wants me to be.

But there is also the fact that I reacted so quickly to his insistence on helping me that I don't even know what his offer to help entails. This doesn't help me feel any better about my reaction to him. Is he really trying to help, no stings attached? Just being generous? Would he have done this with anyone else, or is it just me? Is his help a long-term thing, or only until the baby is born?

For the first time since I told Riley I was pregnant, I consciously touch the pouch between my hips. Chills of delight dance across my skin. I switch hands, placing my right across my belly, and pick up my spoon to take another sip of broth.

Considering it's hospital food, it's really not half bad. But then again, cardboard would probably taste good to me right now. I meant to eat something earlier, when Mikah was here, but I kept falling asleep. I plow through the soup, bread roll, fruit and crackers in what feels like less than five minutes. I still feel hungry, but I don't want to overdo it.

I sit back and pick up the book that Dr. Alston left for me, *What to Expect When You're Expecting*. The cover has a picture of a pregnant woman standing against a blue background, and the back jacket promises that the book will help me understand my body and my baby throughout the various stages of pregnancy. It looks very...clinical.

I open it and start to read. I was right — it is quite clinical — but there are some really cool things in here. Now I understand why my breasts hurt so much. I also learn that the vomiting and exhaustion should start to ease soon. The prospect of this is exciting on so many levels.

Eventually Amanda returns to my room. Once she's satisfied that I ate everything, she pulls me from my bed to walk around the hallway. I'd rather not walk — I'm feeling sleepy again — but she lures me out with the prospect of removing my IV, and I can't resist.

It turns out that I am in the maternity ward. A couple of other women walk the halls, too. Every so often they stop and groan. They must be in labor. I shudder. I'm still trying to come to grips with the fact that I'm pregnant, never mind the prospect of labor or — I shudder again — delivery.

Once we are back in my room, Amanda removes my IV. Another nurse, Jackie, comes in and introduces herself as the nurse on duty tonight. I'm told to push the button if I need anything. She will be back in a few hours to check on me, but for the most part, she'll leave me to sleep.

I say thank you and goodnight to Amanda, who reassures me she'll be back in the morning even if Dr. Alston can't make it.

Once they're gone, I roll onto my side, gently placing my hand upon the small mound. Lying in this position again reminds me of when Mikah was here, his eyes bright green with wonder. I can no longer ignore the fact that I feel horrible for kicking him out. The more I think about it, the more I am convinced he was just trying to help.

I've never had someone willingly want to take care of me the way that Mikah does, and it makes it hard for me to accept without suspecting there is more to it than meets the eye. Riley always paid for everything and I never worked, but I was expected to do things to him and for him in return. But somehow I can't believe can't believe Mikah operates that way. But if I'm going to consider accepting his help, Mikah needs to back off from pushing me to do things.

What's more, since that ultrasound and reading some of the stuff Dr. Alston left me, I'm finally beginning to see that this is far bigger than I've allowed myself to realize.

I slowly rub my hand across my tummy. "You give me reason," I whisper, and then I fall asleep.

THIRTEEN

Around ten the next morning, I'm in a cab driven by Chuck - a nice man who's old enough to be my grandfather and who says he's a native of Minneapolis – ready to head back to my apartment. As we're leaving the hospital campus, a really nice, sleek black Mercedes drives into the lot next to us. I can't be certain, but I think it's the same one I saw in my neighborhood on Thursday night. And I'm pretty sure it's Mikah driving.

I toss the thought aside. I don't want to hope that maybe he was coming back to see me. Or that it was even really him to start with.

Fifteen minutes later, we are pulling up in front of my apartment. I reach into my bag to pay Chuck, but he stops me. "The hospital takes care of it," he says, smiling warmly. I try to tip him and he refuses that, too. Instead he helps me from the car and stays standing near the rear passenger door until I'm inside my building.

Once inside my apartment, I start to feel tired again and consider resting for a bit. But as much as I want to lie around all day, I have laundry – and now grocery shopping – to do. Better to stick to my routine.

I gather up my laundry bag and empty the contents of my hospital bag into it. I'm wearing a pretty cool pair of light purple scrubs Amanda found for me. The top is huge, but the pants are really comfortable. I leave the pants on and swap the shirt for a white t-shirt that used to say *meh* across the chest but has since faded. After taking a good look at my tummy during the ultrasound yesterday, I've realized that I'm going to start needing clothes here really soon. Most of the bottoms I own are pajamas or sweatpants with an elastic waistband, so those I know can wait to be replaced, but shirts are going to become a problem.

Once my laundry bag is packed, I grab a small envelope off of the fridge. It is addressed to my landlord and already has a stamp on it. I place the four money orders of a hundred dollars each inside — I got them when I cashed my check at the bank, like I do every payday — seal it, and throw it into my bag.

I pull out the wad of cash from my wallet. All in all, there are about two hundred and thirty dollars here, but I don't need to be walking around these streets with this much cash. I pull out forty dollars, place the rest between the pages of my journal and put it back under my bed. I also grab the food stamps and the list of approved foods to look over while doing laundry and head out the door.

As I step outside, I throw my laundry bag sling-style across my back, over my purse. I look like Rambo with bag straps instead of belts full of bullets.

It's a little cloudy out today, and there is a fall chill in the air. I pull my hood up over my head and start walking the two blocks to the Laundromat. This time of day is nice. Sometimes people even say hi. No one says hi today, but I get some nods and smiles — which I return — from some of the people sitting or standing around outside their homes or shops.

I get to the Laundromat and head over to load my card with enough for wash and dry, plus detergent. Find a washer, load it, start it and sit back to wait.

My stomach grumbles. I pat my tummy. Having eaten so much in the last day or so is going to make it hard to not eat. It's only eleven in the morning and I just ate breakfast three hours ago, but I'm hungry again. I let out a sigh and decide that I can afford something from the coffee shop next door, so I get up and head over there.

"Hi, Ms. Wilson," I say to the elderly woman coming in the door. She is here this time every Saturday. Most mornings we talk - about nothing really, but the company is nice in a boring old Laundromat. Ironically enough, she reminds me of Mrs. Wilson from those Dennis The Menace cartoons.

"Hello, Vivienne. How are you today?" she asks.

"Better, thanks. I was going to go next door for a bagel. Would you like something?"

"Oh, no, dear. I have toast. Go have fun. Are you using your usual machine?" I nod. "I'll keep an eye on it."

I smile because I can't even begin to imagine the things she would do if someone was trying to steal my clothes. "Thanks, Ms. Wilson."

The coffee shop is decorated like a junkyard. There are tons of eclectic metal objects, from sculptures to wheels and old hubcaps. The furniture and tables are all mismatched, too, but in some strange way, it all works. There are a couple of computers lined up along the wall with a sign overhead that says, *Up to 1 hour free.*

The girl behind the counter is wearing a spiked dog collar, short jean shorts with pink-and-black striped leggings underneath, and a black fishnet shirt over a thin white t-shirt. The fishnet on her arms is ripped, and her black bra is visible beneath the t-shirt. It's a look that I thought had died about ten years ago, but she manages to pull it off spectacularly. It compliments the massive, six-inch-long Mohawk she's sporting.

"Hi, there, what can I get for you?" she asks in an overly friendly tone. The black lipstick she's wearing cracks when she smiles.

"Hi. Just a bagel, plain."

"Sure thing. Anything else?"

"A large glass of ice water."

She rings it up and grabs my order.

"Can anyone use those computers?" I ask as she hands me my change. I don't want to be told to get up if I sit down.

"Absolutely. You have one hour, but unless we get really busy, take as long as you like."

"Thanks."

I grab my water and bagel and head toward the computer on the end. I'm not super familiar with computers, but I know how to search the internet, and that's all I need to know today.

I sit down and jiggle the mouse, and the screen flickers to life. Clicking on the browser icon opens up to Google. I type in two words: Mikah Blake.

Thousands of results pop up in a matter of seconds. There's everything from his company to random news articles. I munch absently on the bagel as I start with the homepage for MSB Enterprises. Sure enough, there is a picture of Mikah. It's a formal picture, and he's not smiling. He's barely recognizable this way. I read his bio.

Born Mikah Shannon Blake, 1987, Dublin, Ireland. He's a little younger than I thought. Well at least I was right about the subtle Irish accent. *Mr. Blake moved to the*

Boston area in 1990— My jaw drops. He was in Boston the year I was born. *—with his father and mother, who later had three additional children, two boys and one girl.*

I continue scanning the rest of the bio. I was right about the Ivy League education: *Mr. Blake graduated from the MIT Sloan School of Management in 2009 with a Master of Finance (MFin).* Holy crap, he was only twenty-one when he received his Master's degree. My age. Wow!

The last sentence captures my attention. *Mr. Blake is the youngest entrepreneur to make it into Forbes 500.* This explains a lot. Mikah is a very driven individual; I have no doubt that he will stop at nothing when it comes to something he wants. I smile slightly at the events that led up to yesterday's hospital visit.

I hit the back button and move on to some more articles. I finally find one that captures my attention, dated April 16, 2011. *CEO of MSB Enterprises, Mikah Blake, buries father, two brothers in Boston.*

"What in the world?" I click the link.

Mikah Blake attended funeral services at St. Ambrose in Boston this afternoon for his father, Shannon, age 48, brother Shane, age 20, and brother Ronin, age 17. All three were killed when their vehicle was hit by a semi-truck going the wrong way down Highway 95 Tuesday last week....

I can't read anymore; my eyes are swollen and tears are falling down my cheeks. I click the button to go back to the search results. The next two or three pages are filled with more articles about his father and two brothers. I finally come across one that says something about his sister, Victoria.

Victoria Blake, younger sister to CEO Mikah Blake, was admitted to Boston Medical Center early yesterday morning after an apparent suicide attempt.

I don't need to read any further. I click the back button again, but not before I catch the date on the article: April 11, 2011. Just before the funeral for his father and brothers.

Bottom line in my research today: Holy crap. I never, ever expected to find that. My heart aches.

I close the browser window, grab my water, pop what's left of my bagel into my mouth and place the plate on top of the garbage can.

"Thanks for coming," the girl behind the counter says.

"Thank you, have a good day."

"You, too."

After finishing up with my laundry, I decide to head back to my apartment to drop off my clean laundry so I don't have to haul it around the grocery store, which is in the opposite direction from my apartment as the Laundromat.

As I stomp up the stairs, I notice a piece of paper stuck in my doorjamb. I grab the note and go into my apartment, locking the door behind me. The handwriting is sloppy. So different from Mikah's tidy penmanship.

Vivienne,

I stopped by just to make sure you made it home okay. Looking forward to seeing you in two weeks.

Dr. Anne Alston

Okay, this is getting a little bit creepy.

Something on the floor catches my eye: another envelope. No address, and this one is thicker. Weird.

I pop the seal. Inside are the ultrasound pictures that Dr. Alston took yesterday. The first one has a Post-it note attached to it: *These were left in the emergency care ward by accident when we moved you.*

Odd that I hadn't even thought about them. Pulling them out, I look at them again. It is still so hard to believe that this little guy — or girl — is growing inside me. Flipping through the pictures, I notice that there are only seven of them.

"What the hell?"

I check the envelope again, but there is nothing else inside. One picture is missing.

"Who would want someone's ultrasound picture?"

But even as I ask myself that question, the image of one beautiful face comes to mind. Mikah Blake.

FOURTEEN

On Monday morning I meet with a really nice lady named Jessica at the W.I.C. office. She tells me that it usually takes weeks to get into their office, but because Dr. Alston had called, saying that it was an emergency, they were able to see me right away.

She explains the program to me and I sit through an orientation class about the W.I.C. process. Every four weeks I can come back to pick up new vouchers for various foods. It seems like way too much food for one person. I know it's not true, but I feel like I'm taking the food away from someone else who really needs it.

On Tuesday I swing by the nursing home to see my mom. She's the same as ever: She just sits there staring out the window, seeing nothing. I ask myself why I go out of my way to visit her, and the only answer I can give myself is that she's my mom.

We didn't have the best relationship — if you can even call it that — while I was growing up. She never saw fit to take care of me, and more often than not, I found myself taking care of her. I got up every day in time for school, went to school, came home, studied, made dinner, cleaned the house, studied some more, and went to bed, only to repeat the process the next day.

Weekends often found me alone in whatever apartment we were staying in while Mom was off with God only knows who, doing God only knows what. Usually she'd stumble home late Sunday night or sometime during the day on Monday and pass out for a couple of days. Then she'd be right back at it again.

I learned to steer clear of her when she ran out of money. She had a venomous temper and would storm around the house yelling and throwing things. Sometimes she would hit me just because I asked a question. At the time, I didn't understand what I'd done to deserve it. I understand better now that she was unable to control her own anger, and her means of coping were always drugs or alcohol.

On my way home from visiting my mother, I stop at the grocery store again, picking up some repeat things, and some new. I discovered very quickly after cooking up some chicken Saturday night that chicken does not sit well with me — I threw it up — so chicken's out. I look at the store's selection of red meat, and my stomach turns. Hm. Evidently all meat is out for now. I'll talk to Dr. Alston next week about some alternative options.

For the moment, macaroni and cheese, peanut butter and jelly sandwiches, and scrambled eggs seem to be my foods of choice, and I'm okay with that.

Wednesday and Thursday pass quickly without incident; all I do is work, eat and sleep.

But Friday night at the diner is strange. It's extremely busy — which is nice because it passes the time quickly — but only a few of our regulars are here. The rest are classier, well-dressed and well-behaved people who look like they'd be more comfortable in a swank hotel bar than in Bertie's shitty little diner. Laura chalks it up to something happening downtown. It still seems odd to me, but I can't complain. I leave work at around twelve thirty with over three hundred dollars in tips — something that is completely out of the ordinary. Happy with the fact that I've managed to make more than half of my rent in one night, I head home.

Once again, Al is behind the wheel. We have our typical conversation and I notice that I don't feel anywhere near as tired as I was just a week ago.

"You're looking well," Al says when we're almost to my stop.

"Um, thanks," I say, confused.

"No, I mean it. Have you gained some weight?"

I think back to putting on my uniform before work and realize he must be right. "I'm trying," I say.

"Keep it up."

He drops me at my stop and lingers until I round the corner. As soon as the bus moves on, headlights appear behind me, casting my shadow across the pavement and illuminating my path. The vehicle isn't moving. I quicken my pace, my heart pounding.

I push on the door to my building, and as I slip inside, the car drives by. A black Mercedes.

Inside my apartment, I drop my mail on the counter, strip off my uniform and head toward the shower. I stop to check myself in the mirror – something I haven't really done since before the trip to the hospital – and I suddenly see what Al was talking about.

My eyes are a lighter, brighter blue. My cheeks are still a little hollow, but they seem to be filling out a bit. And I don't look quite so pale. Though my collarbones are still visible beneath my skin, they're a little less pronounced. The biggest shocker are my breasts, which seem a lot fuller. Not bigger, just fuller. And my nipples are a few shades darker than they used to be.

I look down my body to the bump between my hips. It too is more rounded and softer looking, though my hipbones are still well defined. I gently caress the bump with one hand as I remove the hair tie from my bun with the other, letting my hair cascade down my back.

I turn on the shower, all the way to the hottest setting, and pray. It's warmer than usual, so I jump in, but I barely get my hair washed before the water starts to run cold. I move quickly and hop out. For once in my life I'd love to take a shower that is hot and stays hot for as long as I want.

As I towel off, I notice that I'm moving more gingerly than I used too. I'm a little more cautious in my movements. After I get into my pajamas, I make myself a pb&j with grape jelly and grab the book Dr. Alston gave me. Flipping to the section on week twelve, I start to read by the tiny lamp near my bed.

While reading, I realize that Dr. Alston seems to be spot-on with her assessment of how far along I am. Over the last couple of days my breasts have switched from being painful to feeling heavy, my tiredness seems to be waning slightly, and I'm beginning to feel my energy level rising. I'm also hardly ever hungry. But then again, these days, if I feel hungry, I eat —something I've never done in my life. I'm beginning to wonder how I survived this long.

FIFTEEN

I'm running through our apartment. He's right on my heel, chasing me.

"Abigail, get her!" he says.

"You want her, you get her," my mother shouts from another room.

Suddenly I'm flying backwards. The pain in my scalp surges through my body and I go limp. I'm being dragged backwards by my hair into a room along the hallway. Only it's not a room, it's a closet. He pulls my hair harder and suddenly I'm spinning around. A hard, heavy hand comes across my face.

My head snaps back, knocking into the jamb of the closet door. I see stars. He grips my arm so hard it burns. I start to cry. He grabs my other arm just as hard. I can feel the veins popping and burning.

"Get your sorry ass in that closet and stay there."

I can't move because of the grip he has on my arms. Suddenly one of the hands is gone and I can feel him shift his weight. I try to flinch away but his grip tightens further as his hand comes down hard across the same cheek, snapping my head back into the jamb again.

He shoves me roughly into the closet and I stumble, falling to the floor. The door slams shut. Something heavy scrapes along the wall and bumps to rest against the door.

"Now you can't get out."

Panic sets in. I try in vain to open the door. My arms are weak, throbbing from his grip, useless.

"Alright, bitch, you have work to do." His voice comes from down the hall. Then I hear the smack. "Damn it, bitch, get to work."

I start beating on the door, panicked in the dark. I'm hot, I'm alone, and I'm hurt...

My eyes fly open. My heart races, my breathing coming fast and hard. I try to shake the memory, but the adrenaline is still pumping through my veins. It hadn't been the first time I'd been locked in the closet by one of my mother's drug dealers or pimps while they beat and fucked her, but on that occasion I'd spent at least three days in that closet before the paramedics finally showed up.

It never made sense to me that she kept going back to those types of men. Did she enjoy the beatings? Get off on them? The thought makes me queasy. Maybe she just didn't know how to do things any different. Maybe she didn't know they *could* be different.

Thank goodness I got away from Riley. Even if I was a little late in realizing the importance of pulling away, I did it. Despite the consequences.

Still trembling, I climb out of bed and head into the bathroom.

When I come out I feel calmer. The clock next to my bed reads nearly eleven in the morning. I yawn and stretch, ignoring the little flutter of panic at exposing my belly, and try to decide what to do first.

It's Saturday, laundry day. I consider skipping it — I still feel unsafe after that dream and laundry means going out in public — but one look around my apartment at the dirty clothes strewn about tells me I don't have much of a choice. I bend down and start stuffing clothes into my laundry bag.

The intercom buzzes. My heart jolts. "Who on earth?"

I push the intercom button. "Who is it?" My voice comes out a little harsher than I intend. I take a deep breath and let it out slowly while a male voice crackles through the intercom.

"My name is Alex. I have a delivery for Vivienne?"

"What is it you're delivering?"

"Groceries," he says back.

What the hell? Do I go downstairs and meet him or stay here and let him up? Not wanting him near my apartment, I tell him, "I'll be right down."

"I was told to bring them up to apartment nine."

Damn it.

Okay, I can let him up and stay behind the door and the chain. It's not much, but at least if he tries to break down my door, other people might hear.

I buzz him into the building.

After a moment, I can hear someone climbing the stairs. He sounds heavy. My heart starts pounding. He gets closer. Then I hear him take the two steps across the landing to my door.

Knock, knock. "Vivienne, it's Alex."

About now I really wish I had a peephole. I unlock the deadbolts and the knob but leave the chain. I open the door a crack. On the other side is a boy, really, not much taller or bigger than I am, wearing a Cub Foods shirt and carrying a paper bag with the Cub logo on it.

The panic settles a little, but I'm still cautious. "Who sent the groceries?" I ask him.

"A gentleman by the name of Mikah Blake."

I curse under my breath. "Send them back. I don't need them."

"He said you'd say that."

"Well, take them back, then tell him if he insists on my having them, he can deliver them himself."

He chuckles. "He said you'd say something like that too, so he told me to give you this." He slips me a piece of folded paper.

I take it from him, keeping my leg pressed against the door, and open it up. Sure enough, it's Mikah's handwriting.

Dearest Vivienne,

If you're reading this I know you're protesting my groceries. I send them with Alex here because I am trying hard to not force myself on you. But I want you to have some of these goodies that I know you won't buy yourself. Please accept this gift as an apology for the way things happened at the hospital.

I hope you're well.

-M

The bottom of the letter has his phone number on it, the same one that's on the back of his card.

"Alright, Alex, you can put the bag down."

"I'm supposed to bring it in and put it away."

"Nope. I'll spare you your job by accepting the bag. You can do me the favor of putting it on the floor and going down to the landing."

He nods skeptically and places the bag on the floor. He slowly backs away to the stairs. When he's on the landing,

I close the door and unlatch the chain. Then I open it again just wide enough to drag the bag inside. Alex is watching me from the landing.

"Thank you, Alex."

"You're welcome."

I watch for a moment as he heads down the stairs, then I shut my door and look into the bag. On top is a bag of goldfish crackers. I shakily remove the crackers and my heart flutters a bit. Below them, a bag of Oreo cookies. My tummy rumbles. Moving the cookies aside reveals a square package, wrapped in silver paper, and the top of what looks like a champagne bottle. As I pull out the bottle, I see it is actually sparkling cider. My heart warms to Mikah just a little more. Then I grab the package. I look in the bag to make sure there is nothing else in it, but there is: a container of beautiful, bright red strawberries. As I lift the container, something on the bottom of the bag catches my eye.

It's a card in a light blue envelope. It says, *Open Me 2nd.*

"Huh?" I huff.

I look back at the package and decide to save it and the card for later, after laundry, when I'm ready to...

I look at the package again. What on earth did he do? My curiosity gets the better of me.

I pick up the package and shake it, hoping that its rattle will tell me what it is. Silence.

I turn it over and slide my finger underneath the seam. Rip off the paper. I'm looking at a plain black box. I raise an eyebrow at it, like it's going to tell me its secrets if I look at it in just the right way. It just sits there.

Well, only one way to find out, I guess.

SIXTEEN

Underneath the lid is purple tissue paper, and underneath the paper is a silver frame holding a picture. My picture. The missing ultrasound picture. The one where the baby looks like it's waving at me.

Tears fill my eyes, making it hard to read the inscription.

Baby Callahan's First Picture
Friday, October 12, 2012

I raise the picture from its resting place in the box. Beneath the frame is another note.

I'm sorry I took this image from you. I know it was your favorite. I wanted to give you something special. -M

My heart clenches as I realize that Mikah is quickly becoming more than I realized. Although I'm a little upset that he took the picture without asking, I'm also flattered.

"You're forgiven," I say aloud, and I wipe the tears from my cheeks. I grab the card and rip it open.

On the cover is a single yellow rose on a white background. Next to the rose in an elegant font it says, *Thinking of you.*

"Why, Mikah? Why me?"

The inside of the card contains a longish note in Mikah's penmanship.

Vivienne,

For reasons I can't explain, I need to be close to you. At least to know you're okay.
I saw something in you that first night that made me think of happier times, times that have long been forgotten.

Seeing your beautiful baby last week made me think about all the things that truly matter in life, and for that I'm grateful.

You give me reason, you give me hope and you give me life. No amount of time will allow me to repay that debt to you, but I'd like the chance to try.
-M

P.S. I know it's not champagne, but I hope you enjoy your cider and strawberries.

P.P.S. Thank you for accepting my gift and for reading my card.

I grab the picture and curl up on my bed, hugging it and sobbing. The picture in the frame is larger than the original. Which makes me wonder where the original is.

As much as I want to accept Mikah into my life, I can't seem to allow it to happen and I don't understand why. I had a panic attack after I kicked him out of my hospital room for crying out loud, but I'm scared.

Despite the fact that he keeps pushing me to accept his help, I'm extremely comfortable around Mikah. Up until now, I've only known Riley and the men my mother kept around, so my instinct is to be afraid. But Mikah brings me such comfort. It's the oddest thing. Somewhere deep down I'm starting to think that not all men can be lumped into the Riley category. Riley stole my innocence and tore up my heart. But Mikah - Mikah seems bound and determined to repair the damage Riley did.

When I smacked him across the cheek, he did nothing more than embrace me, comfort me. He knew instantly what he had done to scare me, and he apologized. Apologized! When I'm the one that hit him!

And in that hospital room, he was nothing but kind and generous. He supported me like no man ever has. He stayed with me and comforted me. He was awed by my baby. And I threw him out. God, I'm such an idiot.

I'm drawn to him, but I can't seem to let myself get close to him. I'm terrified because he gives me so much hope, and I know that if I let my feet float off the ground, I will come crashing back down so hard that I won't recover this time. I'm damaged, I'm broken, and I have permanent scars that not even someone like Mikah can erase.

Maybe Mikah is pure-hearted and has fabulous intentions. He's just picked the one girl on the planet that can't be saved.

SEVENTEEN

On Tuesday I go spend some time with my mom. She's a little more animated, and it's kind of nice to see. On my way out I ask the nurse if she's usually like that - animated.

"No, she pretty much just sits quiet and doesn't say much."

It makes me feel a little bit better knowing that her level of sedation or animation has nothing to do with me.

I've often wondered if she holds me responsible for how her life turned out. I know that it's stupid to think that way, but sometimes, remembering how she let her men treat me, I wonder if she resented me.

On Wednesday I get to work with about twenty-five minutes to spare. When I step off of the bus, I do a double take, my heart seizing in panic. Across the street, moving away from me, is a skinny man with dirty blond hair who looks a hell of a lot like Riley. I know he's in jail so it's stupid to think it could be him, but I scurry quickly into the diner anyway.

Once inside, I see Bartie sitting near the register, his usual spot.

"Hi, Bart," I say. He gets really annoyed if you call him Bartie to his face. He's about five feet eleven inches and two hundred fifty to three hundred pounds. Garrison's Diner has been owned by his family since the early 1900s and is practically a historic landmark in Minneapolis. It's unfortunate that the neighborhood around the diner has gone to pits, but he still stays in business.

I haven't seen Bartie since before the hospital visit, so I'm a bit disappointed that he's here tonight. It also makes me anxious. He's not normally here when I come in, so I instantly start to think he's going to fire me.

"Vivienne?"

"Yes, sir?"

"How are you feeling?"

I suppress the shock I feel at his question. "Great, thanks. How are you?" I begin walking toward him, but stop about five feet away. Though he's never really done anything to make me mistrust him, there's this invisible danger zone around him that sets off my warning bells. Maybe it's my inexplicable desire to please him. Or maybe it's the fact that he's quite the grease monkey when it comes to his clothes and hygiene.

"I'm good. You're looking well. You've gained some weight?"

"I think so. I don't own a scale, so I can't say for sure."

He laughs his awful, too-many-cigarettes laugh. "Well, I can see it. Can you come here, please?"

I'm momentarily dumbstruck, and then I manage to make myself move another couple feet toward him.

"What's up, Bart?" I ask, trying to sound nonchalant.

He lowers his voice. "I just wanted to let you know that Laura and I talked yesterday. You know, about last week." Oh no. "I just wanted you to know that you've done a great job working here. As long as you don't make a habit out of it and we can cover your shift, I will never fire you because of being sick."

Release breath. "I don't plan to make it a habit. More than anything, I really like and need this job."

"I know, and I like having you here." He smiles. His front tooth is severely crooked and he is missing two teeth on the bottom.

"I will remember that. Thank you, Bart."

"Good deal. Now, there is a woman in booth fourteen who asked for you by name. Go change your shoes and help her out, okay?"

I nod and head off, wondering who could've asked for me. The only women I know that would be in this restaurant claiming to know me are Amanda and Dr. Alston. I turn to look, but I can't see over the top of the high-backed booth.

I change my shoes quickly, shed my hoodie and tie up my apron. The top of the apron quickly slips below my belly. Initially I think it makes me look huge, but when I look at myself in the mirror, it's not all that noticeable. Which is good, because despite Bartie's claim, I have no doubt that he would be quick to harass me about it. I've heard stories - even from his own son - about some of the things he's done because someone made him mad. I know I can't hide my pregnancy from him forever.

I can't stop myself from looking at table twelve - Mikah's table - on my way over to the booth next to it. My heart aches at the sight of that empty table, and I suddenly have this need to see him. To thank him and—

My heart stops and my steps falter. Sitting in the booth I'm heading toward is a black-haired girl I had hoped never to see again - Rebecca!

Fear grips my throat as I consider the possibility that it really was Riley outside after all.

Rebecca is Riley's wannabe girlfriend. She thinks he's the greatest thing since sliced bread, and I have no doubt Riley cheated on me with her. He was always saying I was lousy in bed and even made a point a few times of telling me that he'd slept with other women. Rebecca, I'm certain, was one of them.

"What the hell are you doing here?" I snap as I approach the table.

"Well, hello to you, too, Vivienne."

"Answer my question," I say through gritted teeth.

"Is that any way to treat a customer?"

"No, but you are no customer."

She turns her head to look at me. I gasp. Her right eye is purple and swollen shut.

"No, I'm not. I came to warn you."

"Warn me. How the hell did you know I was here in the first place?"

"Word gets around."

"That's funny, because there isn't anybody that knows I'm here."

"Guess again."

This is just damn fantastic. I feel my anxiety level rise dramatically, and I'm suddenly desperate to get her out of here.

"What's your warning?"

It's taking all the self-control I have to keep from giving her another black eye. Another part of me is debating on whether to run out the back door.

"Do I have to explain it to you? Isn't it obvious?" She looks at me full-on, showing off her bruises.

"You have a black eye. What does that have to do with me?"

"Riley gave it to me. To show me what he planned to do to me if I didn't find you and report back to him. When I told him I found nothing, he did it again. And again." She wants sympathy from me. Is she serious?

"Well, he put me in the hospital."

Her jaw drops. "I didn't know that."

"I'm sure you didn't. What I want to know is how and when he got out of jail."

"You know his father. Drug charges are enough to motivate him to act. He bailed him out."

Fucking fabulous. Drug charges. Is she kidding me? "I need to get back to work."

She stands up and I catch the first glimpse of her body. "Dear God, please tell me that's not Riley's," I say pointing to her easily six-month-pregnant belly. She flushes and looks down coquettishly at the floor. "Whatever you do, don't tell him that. I'm surprised you've managed to get away with it this long without him figuring it out," I whisper, remembering his reaction. I gently place my hand on my little mound. "That's how I ended up in the hospital."

In an instant, she starts crying. "I'm sorry, I didn't know."

"Get out of here, Becca, and get away from him," I say in a tight voice.

"I can't."

I feel a surge of pity as understanding washes through me. Becca's situation is not much different than mine was. Walking away isn't easy.

Neither of us says anything, and after a moment she leaves. Once she's gone I go over to Bartie. "Can I have a minute?"

"Sure, but stay close."

"Thanks." I turn to head off toward the bathroom.

Jesus. Becca looks like hell. I'm not sure if I should feel sorry for her or what. I am surprised that he lets her around him; she's easily three months further along than I am. Which confirms that he was cheating on me. Becca, no doubt, is one of dozens of women out there with a Riley stamp on them, knocked up or otherwise. The thought brings chills, and I make a mental note to try and discuss some things with Dr. Alston on Friday.

I suddenly feel very dirty. I wash my face and arms, trying to shake the feeling.

It's a slow night, and around eleven, the cook, Bart Jr., or BJ, who also happens to be Bartie's nephew, tells me to take off early. I look at Nyssa for reassurance and she nods.

I step outside just in time to catch the next bus. As I'm climbing on board, I catch a glimpse of a man with slick, black hair and nice threads walking into the diner. He looks a lot like Mikah. But the bus takes off before I can ask the driver to let me out. I consider getting off at the next stop and walking back, but the next stop is a ways down the road; by the time I get back to the diner, he'll have left.

About forty minutes later we get to my stop. This driver isn't Al, so he doesn't linger. Right before I turn the corner, headlights come on across Lake Street, shining on me from behind. By the time I get to the door the headlights have moved on, just like the other times. And just like the other times, I look over my shoulder to see a sleek black Mercedes.

I'm exhausted tonight, so I forgo my shower and climb into bed, bringing the bag of goldfish crackers with me.

I smile at the thought that Mikah just might be trying to disobey my order to leave me alone, and then find myself comforted by the idea that it's him in the Mercedes making sure I get home okay. Though I'm wondering how he beat me to my apartment tonight, considering I got home an hour early and he had just been going into the diner when I left. Assuming that was him.

I realize after a few minutes that I've been absentmindedly rubbing my belly and the little bump there. "Maybe one day soon we'll get our timing right," I whisper.

Holy crap, I'm talking to my stomach again. I smile and roll over, reaching for the light. Right before it goes out, I catch a glimpse of my baby waving at me.

EIGHTEEN

Knock, knock, knock.

I groan. I don't want to wake up.

Knock, knock, knock.

"Who is it?" I say groggily.

"Vivienne, it's Mr. Crowley from downstairs."

"Yes?"

"I have a Detective Stevens with me to see you."

My eyes snap open.

In my mind's eye: an image of Detective Stevens sitting in a chair toward the foot of my hospital bed while he asked me questions about Riley. I'd expected him to make me feel like an idiot, to tell me that if I'd been smarter and left sooner, I would never have ended up where I was. But he didn't. Instead he helped me see that I was really a victim, not some dumb girl that didn't know any better.

He is the first cop I've ever come to respect. He's the one who caught and arrested Riley, and I trust him completely.

Come to think of it, he's the first *man* I've ever respected or completely trusted.

But what on earth is he doing here?

"Just a minute," I bark as I scramble out of bed. I really have to pee, but I doubt the detective is going to wait much longer.

I unlock the knob and two deadbolts, leaving the chain in place, and crack open the door. Sure enough, it's the same detective from the hospital.

"Thanks, Mr. Crowley," Detective Stevens says.

"No problem. You okay, Vivienne?" I nod. "Okay, I'll be downstairs if you need me," he says, then heads downstairs.

"What can I do for you, Detective?"

"Can I come inside?"

I hesitate. I don't let anyone in here, ever.

He is quick to sense my hesitation and adds, "I need to talk to you about Riley Bennett and I'd prefer to talk to you in private, if that's okay?"

I feel an emotional waterfall wash over me: hope that maybe he's been picked up again, downright freaked out that I have to once again talk to a cop about Riley, and, finally, fear that something bad is happening.

I shut the door slightly and unhook the chain, then open it back up. A sweet smile spreads across his lips - tender, appreciative. His eyes are looking downward, and panic rises from my toes.

I look down. Sure enough, my tank top is up, exposing a good portion of my bump. "Sorry," I say as I pull my tank top down, and he smiles wider.

"It's a pleasant sight to see, Vivienne. I was worried for you and that little one after we met the last time."

I nod shyly and back up so he can come in. "Listen, I just woke up, can I use the restroom real quick?"

"Of course."

I shut the front door and leave it unlocked. I don't feel threatened by Detective Stevens, and if anyone is going to come in here they can deal with him.

I shuffle off to the bathroom. When I come back out, he is leaning casually against the wall opposite the apartment door, between my bed and the kitchen window.

"What can I do for you, Detective?" I ask again.

"Are you aware that Riley was released last Friday on bail?" he asks, taking a small notebook out of his coat pocket and flipping it open.

I take a deep breath. I expected this when he brought up Riley's name. Hopefully that's all he's here to tell me.

"Sort of. A somewhat mutual friend of Riley's and mine showed up at the diner I work at last night to warn me that Riley was looking for me."

He makes a note. "Which diner?"

"Garrison's."

"Was this friend Rebecca Black?"

I look at him, puzzled. "I think so?"

"About five foot seven, black hair?"

I nod. "That's her."

"What time was she at the diner last night?"

"She was there when I got there at about three forty. She left at about four-oh-five, four ten-ish. Not sure."

"What else did you talk about? Besides Riley's release?" He's fishing for something, but I can't see what, and I'm confused as to why Becca is being brought up in this conversation.

"She had a nasty black eye and told me that Riley had beaten her up, both as an example and because she hadn't given him what he was after."

"What was he after?"

"My whereabouts."

"Why would he want to know that?" There's nothing in his tone besides curiosity.

I shrug, but my stomach is doing flips. "I'm assuming it's to see if he did what he set out to do."

"Which is?"

"I'm sure if you think about why he attacked me that night, you can answer your own question, Detective?"

He nods. "You're right, I could. But what do *you* think?"

"Well, he was after one of two things that night - to kill me, or to kill the baby."

I take a deep breath and shudder as the thought occurs through me that if he'd succeeded in killing the baby, he might have succeeded in coaxing me back to him. I might not have ever gotten away from him. I push the thought away.

"Couple that with the fact that he was thrown in jail, his father is probably pissed that he had to bail him out. Probably threatened to cut him off. Who knows what's driving Riley this time. It doesn't take much to set him off. Most men would have walked away from a pregnant girl, not beat the shit out of them."

He nods and writes something down.

"Believe me, if I'd known that was the reaction I was going to get, I would have never told him. I expected him to be angry, or demand an abortion, but never did I imagine that he would beat me to the extent that he did. I warned Rebecca of that last night."

The detective's eyes widen and his nostrils flare.

"What aren't you telling me, Detective?"

"I'm not at liberty—"

"Don't give me that bullshit. Riley got to Becca too, didn't he?"

He hesitates, then nods.

"So why aren't you questioning her?" I stop. Cold shivers rake through my body. "She told him..." Can't breathe. "He killed her?"

I put my hands on my knees. I hear a strange noise, and it takes me a moment to realize that it's me, gasping for air.

"Relax, Vivienne. Calm..." He has moved to stand next to me. His hand is gently stroking my back.

I'm hyperventilating again, too panicked. I fall to my knees. The jolt of pain causes me to gasp, and suddenly I can breathe again. I begin to calm.

"That's it," he says as I take long, deep breaths and pull myself up onto the bed. "Sorry," he says. "I'm sorry. I didn't mean to frighten you."

I nod, focusing on my breathing. "It's okay," I say between deep breaths. "I'm okay."

Before he leaves, Detective Stevens assures me that there will be officers watching me go to and from work while they try to track Riley down. He says at this point they can't do much except talk to him; when they found Becca, she had high levels of methamphetamines in her system. I never knew Rebecca very well, but Riley certainly wasn't the drug-doing type. Selling, yes; doing, no. Even if she did do drugs, would she do meth while pregnant? She didn't seem high last night when I saw her, but there were more than eight hours between her diner visit and her death.

When I head out for work, I look around and spy a cop car parked down the street, facing my direction. And when I get to work, there's another one coming down the street just behind the bus. I don't linger on the street, just hop into the diner.

NINETEEN

"Hi, guys," I say to Laura and Nyssa as I head back to the lockers. Their answering hellos follow me through the door.

When I come out of the back room, Laura is quick to start asking questions. "There was a Detective Stevens looking for you here today. About gave the old grouch hound a heart attack. Care to tell us what that was all about?"

"Not particularly."

"Are you in trouble with the law?" she is quick to ask.

I laugh nervously. "Seriously, Laura. You think I'm in trouble with the cops?" I am in trouble, of course, just not with the cops. But I'm not sure my co-workers need to know that.

She purses her lips. "No, of course not. But usually when someone doesn't want to talk about why a cop was looking for them, it means they're the one in trouble."

Nyssa laughs a little. "I can't imagine Vivienne hurting a fly, let alone committing some random crime." Nyssa is about the same age as I am, maybe a couple of years older. I know that she works here because she enjoys the job. She is sweet - overly so sometimes, but we get along well. I don't get the motherly vibe from her, but she definitely seems protective.

"Thank you, Nyssa."

"It has to do with the girl that was in here yesterday, doesn't it?" Nyssa says.

My eyes widen as she puts two and two together. "What makes you say that?"

"It was in the *Trib* today. There was a picture of a girl that looked a lot like her. It said something about her being found dead this morning near a dumpster by that old motel down the street."

Oh God. I know my face starts to turn green because the idea makes me want to vomit. "She and I have an old mutual friend. A friend known for beating women," I say quietly.

Laura's shock is almost palpable. "Is this mutual friend why you were in the hospital last week?"

I shake my head, not sure how much I want to tell them. I work with these ladies. Their need to know about my personal life is severely limited, and it already bothers me that Dr. Alston and Mikah know so much. My past is my past and not something that everyone needs to know.

"You know, Vivienne, you can trust us," Nyssa says with sincerity.

I toy with the idea of telling Laura and Nyssa about my pregnancy. I don't want to be sympathized upon, and these two are exactly the two that would do it. Laura in particular will take it upon herself to mother me or find some way to try to take care of me, which would be no different than what Mikah is trying to do. If I knew that their concern would only extend to asking how I was doing, I might feel a little different about telling them more about me. But I realize quickly that explanations might be necessary in order for them to better understand, and the head off future questions.

"Laura, do you remember when I first started working here, and you noticed the bruise on my shoulder while I was changing in back?" She nods. "That was the remnants of an argument between me and the man I mentioned earlier."

They both gasp. This is exactly the kind of reaction I didn't want.

But now that I've started, I find that the words just keep pouring out of my mouth. I tell them about Amber's Place and the social worker who hooked me up with this job. I tell them about Detective Stevens and Rebecca. When I'm finished, I add, "Rebecca's death tells me she made the same mistake I did."

"Which was what, exactly?" Nyssa asks.

"Rather than getting away from him, like I told her to, she went back. I made that mistake too many times, and it put me in the hospital. Nearly killed me."

Both Nyssa and Laura gasp again.

"Stop, both of you. I don't need sympathy or pity. At least that got me out of his grasp and finally on my way to moving on. It's helped me become a stronger person than I was before." I wish I could say the same for Rebecca.

"If you need anything - anything at all - you tell me. Okay?" There is the mother in Laura again.

"Thanks, Laura, but I'm alright."

"So then why were you in the hospital last week?" Nyssa asks.

I sigh. I don't want to go into all the details regarding Mikah and his money, so I just say, "Because the day after I fainted here, I turned around and vomited in a public place. Someone there was worried enough about me to take me to the hospital."

Nyssa was the first to say anything. "I'm glad you went. You were wasting away in front of us. No matter what we did, you wouldn't let us help you."

I blush, sheepish. "You're right. I realize now that I was doing a pretty poor job of taking care of myself, but I've been able to get some more permanent help that's making a difference, and that's what I need right now. But I can't in all honesty say I'd let you help if I needed it. I don't like to be taken care of."

She nods, but I can tell it upsets her. "Nyssa, please know, I've done this my whole life. I've struggled and survived. It's all I know. It's very hard for me to take a handout."

She nods again. "I understand, and I will try hard to remember that." She gives me a hug.

I smile, then frown. "I have a follow-up appointment with Dr. Alston tomorrow morning. She's the one who set me up with food stamps. I've been eating like a pig." I laugh.

"That explains why you've gained so much weight," Laura says.

"Ha! Not that much weight," I retort. Again the idea of telling them about the pregnancy comes to mind, but right now, I'm just not ready to do so. When it's necessary, I will tell them.

"Enough to fill in all of your beautiful features," she says as she squeezes my arm.

"Thanks. Now can we get back to work?" I ask.

And then I realize that Nyssa's shift has been over for a while; she should've been gone when I got here. "Nyssa, are you staying tonight?"

"I stuck around just in case you didn't show up. You know, after the cop was here and all, I wasn't sure what was going on. I'm more than happy to stay if you want to go home."

"No, I'm good. I feel safer here than at my own apartment right now." I shudder slightly. Talking with Nyssa and Laura has been a good distraction from the Riley situation, but now it's at the forefront of my mind again.

Suddenly the bells on the door clink against the glass. We all turn.

TWENTY

When I see Detective Stevens, followed by two cops in uniform, I let out a breath I didn't know I'd been holding.

"Hello, Detective. Who's your friends?"

"Hello, Vivienne. Ladies." He nods his head in their direction, almost like he's tipping his hat to them. "This is Officer Ruiz and Officer Hoffman," he says, pointing to the man and the woman in turn. "We were in the area and thought we would pop in for a bite to eat."

"Wonderful," Laura says, grabbing three menus from the stack. "Follow me."

They dutifully follow her to the one of the tables in the center of the diner. I head behind the counter to wash my hands.

Nyssa follows me over and asks again, quietly, "Are you sure you don't want to go home?"

"No, Nyssa, I'm good. I'll be fine. And besides, you've already been working all day."

She sighs. "I know, but I really want to help you out. Any way I can. I like you a lot, Vivienne, and I..." She trails off. "I just wanted you to know that."

I dry my hands off. "Thanks, Nyssa. I appreciate your concern and your willingness to help me out when it comes to work," I say, remembering that Nyssa saved my skin two weeks ago when Mikah took me to the hospital. I have no doubt that she would do the same again, if needed.

"Vivienne," Laura says, coming behind the counter and reaching for a tray. "I'll grab their drinks, but it's your table."

"That's not necessary," I say back. I'm more and more certain that Laura's been giving me the tables to be nice. Now that the financial burden is not as great as it was even a week ago, I feel self-conscious about continuing to accept all the tables.

"I know dear, but...you know," she says as she scurries off with their drinks.

After the cops are done eating, I take the bill over. "Can I get you anything else?" I say as the door chimes again.

All heads turn in that direction except for mine. The presence of the three cops in front of me is a comfort. If Riley were stupid enough to walk in here right now, these three would protect me.

I look over in Laura's direction. She's smiling toward the door. I look up then, my heart fluttering at the prospect that Mikah might've walked in the door. But it's not Mikah - it's another regular that Laura is friendly with – and my heart sinks.

"No, I think just the check will do," Detective Stevens says.

"Did you guys want it split or all on the same?"

"It's my turn to pay, so just one, thanks," Officer Ruiz says. I hand him the bill. The scowls on the other two's faces are almost comical. Officer Ruiz looks it over quickly, then hands me a fifty dollar bill. "Keep the change."

"Oh no, that's way too much," I say before I can stop myself. I purse my lips, feeling like I've been rude.

"You did a fabulous job, and you had to put up with us. It's not too much." He is smiling warmly at me.

"Thank you." I nod in his direction. "Would you guys like some more coffee?"

They all shake their heads and stand.

"We're good," Detective Stevens says. "Need to get back at it. That was good. Thank you, Vivienne."

"Anytime, Detective. And thank you."

After a short while, we start to get busy. Several tables fill up with customers, and once again we're met with some of the better-dressed, don't-belong-in-this-neighborhood type.

Once the crowd dies down, I tell Laura, "I'm going to go help BJ with the dishes. Holler if you need me."

She scowls at me. I don't normally do the dishes in the back, but I kind of need a break from running around. My feet are a little sore tonight. Plus, washing dishes means that I can stay out of sight for a bit. Each time the bells chime on the door, I jump slightly. I've been getting edgier since Detective Stevens and the officers left, and going to the back will - with any luck - help me relax just a little bit.

After about fifteen minutes, Laura calls back for me and I dry off and head out front. When I come through the door there are five more tables with new people at them. I look at Laura and shrug. Back at it we go.

Around eleven thirty, the diner is finally empty and BJ is out mopping the floor while Laura and I clean up the counter. Filling bottles and sugar containers is boring work, but somebody has to do it.

"Sit," Laura demands.

"I told you, I'm not made of glass and I'm the same person I was yesterday."

"I know, but there is no reason to stand up while you're filling up containers."

"Alright." I take a seat on one of the stools and she slides all the containers my way. I start to marry the ketchup bottles together, then work on the mustard bottles, topping them off and putting them back in the wire baskets that go on the tables.

At some point I realize I'm inadvertently working a little slower than I normally would. Going home is not a high priority tonight like it normally is; the prospect of being at home alone makes my flesh crawl.

TWENTY-ONE

It's a quarter to midnight when Laura says, "Screw it, let's lock up."

I shrug at BJ and head to the door to turn the deadbolt.

I look out the door. No one seems to be anywhere in sight. Not even the cops. As I turn the deadbolt, my eyes spot something across the street in the small space between two shops. It looks white, almost like a t-shirt. It's unmoving. Goose bumps crawl up my arms. I try to shake it off; it's probably just my eyes playing tricks on me.

After we pull down the chairs and BJ shuts down the kitchen, we grab our stuff and head out as a group.

"How long until the next bus, Viv?" BJ asks.

I look at my watch. "About three minutes," I say, heading in that direction. He follows right behind me. On instinct I know that Laura has told him about the detective today. I'm not going to argue.

When I get to the bus stop and turn to BJ, I see that Laura has followed, too. I want to roll my eyes, but I can't deny that I feel safer knowing they're here with me.

I look back to the crevice between the buildings, and the white shirt I thought I saw earlier is gone.

I hear the bus approach from my left. It stops, and the doors swing open. It's Al.

"Hi, darlin'," he says as I climb up. I place my money in the box. "How you doing, sweetheart?"

I smile at him. "Good. Tired, but good."

I look over my shoulder. "Thanks, guys," I say to Laura and BJ. They smile and turn to leave.

I scan the bus, terrified that Riley might be on it. When I realize he isn't, the tension in my shoulders eases by a fraction. Then I noticed a gentleman sitting toward the back. Buzz-cut, dark blond hair, black t-shirt, good looking. Not the type to normally be on this bus this time of night.

I grab the sideways seat behind Al instead of the forward-facing one opposite him. If I need to, I want to be able to make a quick escape.

I look back to the gentleman and he smiles at me. Warm, friendly. Then his hand slides out from behind the seat.

My heart pounds.

I see what's in his hand.

A shield. He's a cop. I start breathing again. He smiles again and nods in my direction slightly. I give him a half-smile in return as my heart rate returns to normal.

A few minutes later, the bus stops to pick up another passenger. I hold my breath again, but it's only a female cop in uniform. "Hi, Al," she says as she climbs up. "How we doing tonight?"

"Great, thanks. Don't usually see you guys this time of night," he says as she slides past the box.

"I'm just taking a ride down the street, back to my car. Had some vandalism at one of the stops, so I've been checking some other ones. No biggy."

She acknowledges me with a nod as she takes the seat I usually sit in, but it's not clear that she knows who I am.

Whether she's been assigned to me or not, I feel safer with two cops on board to protect me.

But she gets off two stops later, and then, at the stop just before mine, the male cop pulls the chain. He stands up as Al brings the bus to a halt, looks at me, smiles.

"Have a good night," he says as he hops down the back door of the bus. I'm not sure why he's decided to get off now.

We rumble up to my stop. "You okay, darlin'?" Al asks as we slow. Maybe he can sense my nervousness.

I nod. "Yup, just tired."

"Have a good night. Be safe out there."

"You do the same," I say as I climb down the front steps. Al lingers until I reach the corner.

Headlights fire up behind me. I'd almost completely forgotten about the Mercedes. The headlights break up as Al passes in front of the car.

I quicken my pace.

The street looks different. It takes a minute to realize why. The light over the door to my complex is out. Great.

As soon as I hit the door to my building, the headlights pass, just like always. I wish I'd thought to find a way to wave down the Mercedes. It's starting to bother me that he's so close yet so far away. I visualize seeing him sitting in the driver's seat, watching me, his beautiful blue-green eyes. Maybe tomorrow I'll call him.

I turn to smile at the car and notice a police car parked in the same spot as this morning. In the dark I can just make out a silhouette in the driver's seat. I give a little wave; it's too dark to see if they wave back.

Stepping inside, I unlock the inner door. Tonight I skip the mailbox and head straight up the stairs. I won't rest easy until I'm locked safe in my apartment.

As I pass Mr. Crowley's door, I notice it's slightly ajar. It's dark inside. He's probably just answering a call from a tenant and forgot to shut his door all the way, but the thought of calling out or going in to investigate makes me scared enough to want to scream. I climb the stairs faster. My scalp prickles as I climb the last flight of steps, and I rub at it.

I reach my door. Do a quick glance around. Nothing jumps out at me or seems out of the ordinary. My heart is pounding, pumping blood through my ears as I place my key in the top lock and turn it. Then the next lock, and finally the knob. I push open the door, letting my breath out in a whoosh.

I'm about to step inside when a hand covers my mouth and nose.

TWENTY-TWO

"Well, well, well...what do we have here. The little whore is all alone."

Riley!

His hand is tight over my nose and mouth, blocking my air. I start to fight back, but he wraps an arm around my chest, squeezing hard.

He pushes me inside my apartment, slamming the door behind us.

I can't breathe.

I claw at his hand over my mouth but my grip is weak and my strength is failing the longer I go without oxygen. I scratch at his arm with my nails.

"Bitch, please. That shit don't hurt. But I have more than a few things that will. At least before I kill you." Panic washes over me as his determination registers.

The next thing I know, he releases me and his hand comes away from my mouth.

I gasp for air.

He pushes me hard.

I bounce off the bed, and then I'm falling toward the floor. I put my hands out, hoping to catch myself before I hit the ground. There is a loud popping sound, and blinding pain races through my body from my right wrist. I cry out and roll onto my side.

Blinking through the pain, I look up and see him looming over me. His dirty blond hair is mussed in short spikes. He's wearing a white t-shirt and black jeans. His eyes are dark, drawn and detached. A look I've seen more times than I care to remember.

"And here I thought this was going to be hard, though I had to deal with your nosey neighbor first."

Mr. Crowley. No. That's why his— No, no, no!

"But yet here you are, just like I like you."

He reaches for my leg. I pull it back and swing hard, narrowly missing his face as he flinches away. The momentum of my kick has sent me rolling back onto my stomach and onto my broken wrist. I scream as pain stabs across my body.

"Bitch!" he says as he reaches once again for my legs.

Before I can react and swing again, he comes down hard with his knee on the back of my leg. "You're mine, bitch! You're going to pay for what you've done to me."

In a flash all of Riley's narcissistic words come rushing back to me. It doesn't occur to him that his own actions put him in jail; it's that I put him there.

"I've done nothing to you." As soon as the words leave my mouth, I brace myself for his retaliation.

Something comes down hard and heavy across the back of my skull. All I can see is brilliant white light.

SNEAK PEEK

Thank you for reading *Give Me Reason.*
Stay tuned for Book 2 in The Reason Series, *Give Me Hope,* coming November 19th, 2013.

Sneak peek of *Give Me Hope.*
***** Mikah *****

"Jesus, God, thank you."

I pull myself up off the floor and take a seat in the front pew, leaning my elbows into my knees.

I feel a vibration along my thigh. My phone. That is about the fifteenth time in the last half hour it's gone off, but frankly, I could care less right now.

Resting my head in my hands, I let the tears flow. They pool into my palms. Breathing deep, ragged breaths, I try to pull myself back together.

I need to go upstairs, but I can't go in the state I'm in. I don't understand why I'm having such a strong reaction to the news about Vivienne. Something I can't explain is happening to me. I need to see her.

"You will see her soon enough."

My head snaps up at the elegant, soft female voice. Nothing. I see nothing.

"You've been chosen to protect her, Mikah. Chosen to see to it that she is safe."

I stand quickly, spinning around. Sharp, blinding pain bounces around my body, and I crumple to my knees.

"What... What is happening to me?" I say aloud.

No response. I ball my fists in frustration, and the pain stops as quickly as it started.

I climb back up into the pew, shaking now because it's not just the pain that's gone but the hum, too. My connection to Vivienne, and it's gone. Panic seeps in.

"Relax."

Relief washes through me in instant response to the command. I have no control over it.

"Why can't you tell me what is going on?"

"Your answers will come in time, when you're meant to hear them."

I feel like I'm losing my mind. I'm hearing voices, talking to myself. Yet I can feel someone with me.

"I am not for you to look upon, young angel. I am here to guide you, to help you into your new life. She is ours to protect and we will. Without fail, we will protect her in the way she is meant to be protected. But we can only initiate the healing; she must do the rest on her own. When the time comes, you will be told what to do next."

"She doesn't want me around," I whisper.

"You do not need to speak aloud, young angel. I know what you think and I feel what you feel. I believe that her life has taken the turn you need to keep her within reach. Do not fret."

I sigh. With the heels of my hands, I press against my temples, trying to dispel the idea that someone is talking to me inside my head. I'm not crazy, am I?

www.ingramcontent.com/pod-product-compliance
Lightning Source LLC
LaVergne TN
LVHW091006080826
845145LV00003B/1144

* 9 7 8 0 6 1 5 8 8 9 1 5 3 *